NICHOLAS ROYLE is the author of more than 100 short stories, two novellas and five novels. His short story collection, *Mortality* (Serpent's Tail), was shortlisted for the inaugural Edge Hill Prize. He has edited fourteen anthologies of short stories, including *Darklands* (New English Library), *A Book of Two Halves* (Gollancz), *The Time Out Book of New York Short Stories* (Penguin), *Dreams Never End* (Tindal Street Press) and *'68: New Stories from Children of the Revolution* (Salt). A senior lecturer in creative writing at the Manchester Writing School at MMU, he reviews fiction regularly for the *Independent* and the *Warwick Review*. He runs Nightjar Press, publishing original short stories as signed, limited-edition chapbooks. Forthcoming publications include a new novel, *Regicide* (Solaris), as well as a collection of short stories, *London Labyrinth* (No Exit Press), and *Murmurations: An Anthology of Uncanny Stories About Birds* (Two Ravens Press). He lives in Manchester with his wife and two children.

## Also by Nicholas Royle:

NOVELS
*Counterparts*
*Saxophone Dreams*
*The Matter of the Heart*
*The Director's Cut*
*Antwerp*

NOVELLAS
*The Appetite*
*The Enigma of Departure*

SHORT STORIES
*Mortality*

ANTHOLOGIES (as editor)
*Darklands*
*Darklands 2*
*A Book of Two Halves*
*The Tiger Garden: A Book of Writers' Dreams*
*The Time Out Book of New York Short Stories*
*The Ex Files: New Stories About Old Flames*
*The Agony & the Ecstasy: New Writing for the World Cup*
*Neonlit: Time Out Book of New Writing*
*The Time Out Book of Paris Short Stories*
*Neonlit: Time Out Book of New Writing Volume 2*
*The Time Out Book of London Short Stories Volume 2*
*Dreams Never End*
*'68: New Stories From Children of the Revolution*

# The Best British Short Stories 2011

*edited by*

## Nicholas Royle

SALT

LONDON

PUBLISHED BY SALT PUBLISHING

Acre House, 11-15 William Road, London NW1 3ER United Kingdom

Printed in the UK by the CPI Antony Rowe, Chippenham

Typeset in Bembo 12 / 13.5

ISBN 978 1 90773 12 9 paperback

Salt Publishing Ltd gratefully acknowledges
the financial assistance of Arts Council England

1 3 5 7 9 8 6 4 2

*To the memory of*

*Giles Gordon (1940-2003)*
*David Hughes (1930-2005)*

# Contents

# Introduction

WE MAY BE living through hard times — for the arts, for anyone relying on any kind of subsidy or support, for everybody really — but there have been harder times for the short story. If I had a pound for every time a writer has complained to me that there is nowhere to send their stories, I'd have enough money to start a new magazine. But in fact there are numerous magazines that regularly publish new short fiction, from literary journals such as the *London Magazine*, *Ambit* and the *Warwick Review* to newsstand titles including *Prospect*, *The Liberal* and the *Sunday Times Magazine*.

Admittedly, most major publishers show very little enthusiasm for the form: some grudgingly allow their more established authors to slip in a collection with their new novel when agreeing a deal, but very few, any longer, will entertain the idea of an anthology of stories by various authors. Faber and Faber will still occasionally launch an author, such as Clare Wigfall in 2007, with a short story collection, but they are the exception rather than the rule. Even more exceptional is Manchester-based Comma Press, a short story specialist, which publishes collections and anthologies with imagination, flair and northern grit. Salt, too, the publisher of the present volume, supports short story writers by continuing to publish collections, and Tindal Street Press, which grew out of a regular gathering of short story writers, the Tindal Street Fiction Group, remains true to its roots.

In genre publishing, the short story retains favoured status. Editors and publishers such as Stephen Jones, Constable and Robinson, Ellen Datlow, Maxim Jakubowski, Peter Crowther/PS Publishing, Andy Cox/TTA Press and others work tirelessly to meet a demand for high-quality short horror, crime, fantasy and science fiction.

There are numerous competitions and prizes, so many in fact that an anthology such as this could easily fill its pages by cherry-picking from the shortlists of these prizes, such as the *Sunday Times* EFG Private Bank Prize, the Manchester Fiction Prize, the BBC National Short Story Award, the Bridport Prize and the VS Pritchett Memorial Prize among others. I made sure to read a number of prize-winning stories while working on the selections for this book. One of them struck me as being very *nice*, very carefully written, but very English, very restrained and reticent. I kept wanting it to reveal itself, to make a run for it, but it kept holding itself in reserve, saving itself. The reveal, when it came, was so timid, so buttoned up, there was a temptation to think, 'Why bother?' All that effort for so little reward.

It's why short stories so often get short shrift from readers, and, consequently, from publishers. Many have little point to them. Picture a figure—a featureless man or woman—standing on a path in a nondescript landscape, the middle of nowhere. The figure starts walking, continues to walk for a bit and then stops. The story ends. The view has barely changed from the walk's starting point. I want my walker to get into difficulty, perhaps face a parting of the ways, speed up, slow down, run for a bit, get out of breath, maybe have to get down on all fours to advance. In front of him or her is a forever retreating summit and beyond that a view we can only imagine until we get there. It may be an epiphany, or a change of heart, or pace or tone; a twist, perhaps, a revelation that calls into question everything that came before. It could be anything, but there's got to be something.

The best stories take you somewhere new, somewhere different, or they take you somewhere you might have been before but by a different route. They help you see the world afresh. They wake you up and make you dream, both at the same time.

I'd rather be left with questions than answers. With a vague feeling of uncertainty rather than one of satisfaction at how neatly everything has been tied up. I'd like the story not to be completely done with in the ten or twenty minutes it takes me to read it. I'd like it to have insinuated itself into my head and taken up residence there for the rest of the day with its questions, its ambiguities. I'd like to find myself remembering it at odd times and wondering whether what I'm remembering is a dream or something that happened before remembering that what I'm remembering is a story.

Having said which, I do want a story to finish, not just to end. Or I want it not just to finish, but to have an ending.

Giles Gordon and David Hughes edited *Best Short Stories*, an anthology series that ran from 1986 to 1994; the publisher was Heinemann. The introduction to their first volume opens: 'This volume has been put together with affection for the most exigent and elegant of prose forms . . .' I would echo that and add that I held and continue to hold enormous affection and respect for the work of Gordon and Hughes.

I had just started seeing my own short stories

appearing in print when the series began and I bombarded the editors with photocopies of typewritten manuscripts in the hope that they would agree that my stories were among the best being written at that time. Fortunately they had the good sense—and taste—to resist my juvenile efforts, responding politely year after year. Eventually, on 2 February 1991, Giles Gordon wrote to me:

> I'm sorry to be returning to you again the stories which you submitted to David Hughes and me for us to consider for this year's BEST SHORT STORIES anthology. In truth, your stories just don't appeal sufficiently to us. They are certainly most competent but they don't, for us, sing out with the necessary individuality and voice. I'd suggest that in future we contact you if we see a story of yours which appeals rather than your going to the trouble of sending stories to us.
>
> Apologies for the typing. I'm stranded at home and my correcting tape has run out.

The funniest and most elegant 'don't call us, we'll call you' letter I ever received—twenty years ago, almost to the day, as I write this.

It was the Gordon/Hughes series that was my inspiration for the present volume, the first of a new series. The main difference between the two series is that Gordon and Hughes picked stories by British and Commonwealth writers, while I am selecting stories by British authors only, wherever they may be based. The stories in this book were first published—whether in print or online—in 2010. It wasn't planned, but as I compare the contents list of the first Gordon/Hughes book with that of the present volume, I see that two names appear in both: Christopher Burns and Dai Vaughan. One or two other writers on my list were represented in later volumes, although some were barely walking when the 1986 volume appeared.

A surprising consistency between the two volumes is that neither features anything reprinted from *Granta*, perhaps the only UK literary magazine that might be named by the man or woman in the street. Gordon and Hughes went on to pick several stories from *Granta*, but I found nothing that grabbed me in the four issues that came out in 2010. Indeed they included very few short stories by British writers. There were memoirs, essays, novel extracts (is there anyone, among readers, writers and editors, who finds a novel extract in any way welcome or useful?) and stories mainly by writers from the US, Pakistan or Spanish-speaking countries. On the evidence of 2010, and the issues that I read in a university library since the magazine failed to respond to requests for copies, *Granta* offers very little support to British short story writers, which is a great shame. Maybe 2011 will be different.

Poet and translator Michael Hulse has a good eye for a story: three of the stories in this book are reprinted from the *Warwick Review*, which he edits. Two appeared first in the *Sunday Times Magazine*, where deputy editor Cathy Galvin oversees the fiction slot. I make no apologies for selecting two stories by Hilary Mantel, each published in a different section of the *Guardian*. Other magazines represented include the *London Magazine*, *Ambit*, *Wasafiri*, *Riptide* and *New Welsh Review*. Perhaps I ought to seek the reader's indulgence over my selection of one story first published by my own small press: Alison Moore's story appeared in the first instance as a chapbook from Nightjar Press. I am merely following the example of experienced editors Ellen Datlow and Stephen Jones who have both reprinted stories from their own original anthologies in best-of-the-year volumes they also edit.

Of course, these stories are the best *in my opinion* and who's to say I'm right? I remember the words of my English teacher, the late Peter Craze, as he responded to the latest of my cocksure outbursts: 'Yes, Nick, literature *is* a matter of opinion, but you're wrong and I'm right.'

Still, I believe this book demonstrates that the short story in Britain today is in excellent health and I hope that readers will agree.

—NICHOLAS ROYLE
Manchester
February 2011

## DAVID ROSE

# Flora

I CAME ACROSS her first in Kew Gardens. I watched her scrambling over the rocks of the rockery, and wondered how long it would be before a warden (are they called wardens? Not guards, surely) remonstrated with her.

Strangely, none did.

A little later, she was in the Alpine House, peering at a saxifrage on the Arctic bench, notebook and pencil in hand. I contrived to peep over her shoulder. She was sketching it, not merely noting its name in the manner of most botanical tourists. The sketch was most accomplished, in my humble opinion.

Later still, she was back on the rockery, sitting on a slab, her feet in the stream, plimsolls by her side, sketching a contorted pine. This time, after a few minutes, she *was* cautioned by one of the staff. She tossed her hair, picked up plimsolls and rucksack and walked away barefoot across the grass.

I completed my seasonal tour of the woodland beds, then went to the Orangery for a little sustenance.

I have never believed in Fate, although I have several times been tempted. But there, in my carriage on the train home, she was. Feet—sans plimsolls—on the opposite seat, a hibiscus blossom, picked, I surmised, in the Tropical House, braided into her hair.

She was blissfully unaware of my disapproval.

I was preoccupied in the weeks after my visit to Kew. I had discovered a fungal infection on a Japanese maple which—the nub of my concern—is host to a rare codonopsis, one I had (I'm boasting here) grown from seed brought back from China.

I spent anxious days swabbing the bark with softsoap and water, checking morning and evening for any fresh irruption.

Yet even as I swabbed and scrubbed, I had to admit to a sneaking regard for the fungal growth—not only its persistence, but its own strange beauty, the subtlety of its opalescent colours, the intricacy of its structure. Are we right, I wondered, to divide Nature as we do?

Nonetheless it had to go, in deference to the codonopsis. Anxious to implement some prophylactic measure, and as my modest library had exhausted its usefulness, I went to the local reference library.

Needless to remark, there she was, still barefoot, her hair, draped over one shoulder, curtaining the book over which she was hunched.

I went on to the next bay, Pests and Diseases. I removed several books *en bloc* for perusal, and noticed that through the resulting gap, I could observe her at her desk. Her posture was one of total concentration. Her stationary arm, deeply tanned, pointed toward me. The elbow was rough, dry, white against the tan. From propping up bars, perhaps. But that, on reflection, was prejudice, for which I mentally rapped my knuckles.

In fact, on further reflection, I realised that what I had caught in myself was closer to tenderness, almost pity for that nonchalantly uncared-for patch of skin.

I took my pile of books over to the furthermost desk and arranged them into a little wall.

They turned out to be limited in scope. My best option was to consult the bibliographies and order the most promising titles commercially. I whittled down the list to an economically feasible number and came away. I think she was still there. Appeared, in fact, not to have moved.

Such is the demand for quasi-academic textbooks that it was some weeks from my initial enquiry before I was able to collect them. I went straight round after receiving the bookshop's postcard (I rarely answer the telephone).

She was — I had almost expected it — there, in the Botanical recess. As I waited for the assistant to locate, price and wrap my books, she came to the counter. She was holding a copy of Wilson's *Flora Pyrenaica* from the second-hand section, but judging from the binding, it was the 1907 edition.

Hesitantly, I said, You do realise there is a later edition, superior to that? Your edition is incomplete; it suffered a partial appendectomy in the printing. Do they not have a copy of the 1912 edition secreted somewhere? Let me ask for you.

She finally looked up.

She said, This is okay. I only need the illustrations. And it's cheap.

I said, You're on a budget? Student, then? Where are you studying?

She gestured vaguely. Up at the College. Holloway.

Botany? I understood they had closed the Botany department. They have sold off the Botanical gardens, I know.

Oh, it's rumoured.

What does your course comprise?

A little of everything.

A foundation course?

I suppose so. But I want to concentrate on botanical illustration.

I thought of the fungus, and the little patch of dry skin.

I said, The departmental library — doesn't it have the Wilson in any edition?

I don't think they have the library now. Perhaps it was sold with the gardens.

I said, That's scandalous. But look, I have a modest library at home. You would be most welcome to use it. It would save your book grant. I take it you have a book grant?

I gave her my card. It was slightly dog-eared from my wallet. I rarely have cause to give them out. But she didn't seem to notice, just tucked it into her book.

We had settled into a spell of fine weather, so I was spending more time in the garden. I even had time, between tasks, to admire the results of my work, to enjoy the garden as a visitor might. The maple was showing no sign of further infection, and the codonopsis insinuated through it was budding nicely.

As I raked the gravel of the dry pond in the Japanese section, the sun was setting, the light sifted through the black bamboo, shadowing the stupa. The breeze stirred the windchimes.

I crossed to the bench in the Mediterranean section to catch the last of the sun before beginning my watering regime. My footfall in the gravel released the scent of lavender and cistus, and suddenly I felt absurdly happy. Also, a sense of—privilege, I would have to call it—that I was able to enjoy all this. I felt obligated to share it all; that my work was in vain if it were all for myself.

I looked across into the sunset, watching the bronze heron as it sank into the dark.

Next morning it was raining.

I answered a knock at the door around midday. She stood, one foot on the step, the other still on the path. Her hair was gathered into a single braid which hung round her neck and over one breast.

I waved her in.

She said, I'm so sorry to intrude. I just wondered. Do you happen to have *Orchidaceae of the Amazon Basin*?

I noticed then that she had a faint accent which, despite my years of travel, I couldn't place.

I said, As it happens, I have.

I led her into the sitting-room–cum–library.

As I unlocked the glass of the book-case, I could see her peering in.

You have *The Clematis in Western Culture*.

Yes. First edition, as it happens. With the hand-coloured frontispiece.

And *Plant Hunting in Nepal*. Where did they come from?

Oh, one collects, you know. Over the years.

I don't normally use the formal construction, but there are times when one finds it appropriate. I handed her the orchid book. She went to put it into her bag.

Ah, I said, as you may have gathered, this copy is quite rare. I can't really allow . . . . You understand?

She coloured charmingly.

You are welcome to use my desk. Stay as long as you wish.

She sat at the desk, unpacked sketchbooks and a pencil case embroidered with beetles. I left her to it.

To mitigate any abruptness in my tone, I took her in a tray of coffee and chocolate digestives. She was immersed in her copying.

Around five, she put her head round the door, to say she was going. I showed her out, and insisted she returned. To show I meant it and in token of my trust, I showed her the spare key to the bookcase. I said, This will be hanging in the hall by the clock. I want you to use it. Books need airing, after all.

I watched from the window as she walked up the street. And as she was met at the corner by a friend. A man, I realised, with a short pony tail, so short as to be almost a pig tail. In my years abroad I had encountered such fashions, years before they were commonplace here. Likewise the anklet above his sandal.

They embraced in the street, in the manner of the young.

Despite my broad-mindedness, I did think to check the library. The book was neatly closed on the desk, the chair exactly in its place.

She returned the next morning. We both smiled as she took down the key. I had left a tray of milk and biscuits on the desk, in case.

The sitting-room-library was originally dining- and

sitting-rooms until I had them knocked through. The serving hatch was now unused, but I hadn't bothered to have it bricked up. Open, as it now was, I caught a glimpse of her arm, sleeved, moving at her work.

After she had gone, I could tell from the disturbance of the books what she had been copying. She had gone on to the genus Convolvulus.

I said, before she settled down for work the following morning, Why not work from real life? I have a *Convolvulus mauritanicus* in flower on the Alpine bed.

She followed me out.

I had a camp stool waiting, but she turned it down, squatted cross-legged on the grass with her sketch book on her knee.

She came back mid-morning for her snack. I had realised that milk and biscuits were hardly suitable, and laid out martini, buttered crackers and a dish of olives. As I brought it in, she began to enthuse over the garden. She said I hope you didn't mind me poking about, but it's all so lovely, like a miniature Kew.

I said, Not at all, I'm delighted to share it. Come and go as you please. Bring your boyfriend sometimes.

Oh, he's not my boyfriend.

Just a chum? Bring him anyway. I will arrange to leave the gate unbolted between ten a.m. and eleven p.m.

She blushed and bent to her books.

He turned out to be considerably older on closer view, or as close as my kitchen window allowed. Still, they made a nice couple as they foraged in the garden.

A week later, she handed me a package as she unpacked her bag. I unwrapped it carefully as she watched. It was a painting of the *Convolvulus mauritanicus*, in ink and water-colour, in an antique frame.

I said, Thank you so much, it's charming. Your own?

I couldn't read the signature, and besides, I didn't know her name.

She said, Yes, but framing it was Jerome's idea.

I said, Thank him for me. It's just right. How clever of him.

She reached for the key of the bookcase. Evidently she had exhausted—temporarily, I hoped—the profusion of my garden.

The desk, she said, you've moved it.

Only a foot or so. I thought it would give you more leg room.

I left the tray on the side table.

Now, with the serving hatch open, I could see her entire. The scuffs on both elbows, the down on her neck, the vertebrae above her top. But someone loved her and I was glad of that.

The fine weather persisted and often, after her work in the library, I would catch glimpses of her, sometimes them, sitting on the benches or strolling in the sun. I had dug out my old birdwatching Zeisses, and could see them comfortably from the bedroom window. She would bend and stroke the foliage on her cheek while he stooped to check the name-plates. Fortunately I was confident of their accuracy, since it had crossed my mind that he may have been her tutor. Such things are not unknown. Certainly he seemed protective.

There was an incident one afternoon—I was in the

kitchen, binoculars not to hand — when I heard a little scream, or maybe a moderate cry. All I could make out was him stamping, almost viciously, on something on the grass. I was at a loss to work out what it could have been. A slug which had somehow evaded my beer traps? But slugs are no more than an irritation to a botanist, although I as a gardener would be dismayed at one.

I searched that evening for some squashed remains but found none, only the outline of something lozenge-shaped and sharp stamped into the lawn.

That, I realised later, was the last time I saw him.

She, after a few days, was back as before, working quietly in the library, her arms more tanned but still scuffed at the elbows. Her concentration was even stronger, and she was taking from the bookcase more and more titles, but always returning them to the shelves as she finished with them. I guessed she was completing a project, up against a deadline. Such was the pressure on her time that she didn't even consume the contents of her tray, except for the martini.

This continued for several days. I thought it better not to break the rhythm of her work, and she came and went ungreeted.

Then she stopped coming. A week had elapsed, then a fortnight, then I knew she wouldn't be back. Her project, I assumed, was finished or she had exhausted my library.

I confessed to a slight hurt that she hadn't said goodbye. I had the framed convolvulus, of course, but I felt that a word of thanks or goodbye wouldn't have been amiss.

The library felt heavily empty when I finally went in. The desk was tidy, the chair straight, the books back in order in the bookcase, or almost. One—*The Clematis in Western Culture*—was out of alphabetical sequence.

I took it out. Between the pages at the top, like a minuscule bookmark, was a hair. I pulled it out, held it to the light. It curled and wiggled with static, clung to my cuff.

I sat at my desk with the book, fingering the embossing and the scuffed buckram edges of the boards. I began to lose myself in the index, in the neutrality of the Latin.

As I laid the book down flat, it began to open to the middle, the illustrations flapping past like a lantern slide show.

I had suddenly to catch a page, turn back. The *Clematis integrifolia* didn't look right. It shouldn't have tendrils—it's herbaceous.

I looked closely. The tendrils had been added to the engraved plate in pencil. They were almost obscene in the outline they limned.

I hastily took down other books I had noticed her using. In *Terrestrial Orchids of the World*, I found a *Cypripedium reginae* with its bladder flower grossly distended, a *Paphopedilum* whose freckles had been added to and a waxed moustache imposed. In Sutton's *Primulaceae*—the original monochrome edition—a *Primula flaccida* had extra stems, wiltingly arched, and a *Primula hirsuta* a clump of frondlike hair drawn in at the base.

I couldn't open any more.

I piled them on the desk and fell into the chair.

The books were stacked with the bottom edges facing me. All of them had a letter inscribed in red—a W on the Sutton, N on *Orchidaceae of the Amazon Basin*, L on *The Clematis in Western Culture*. I was now as much curious as distraught.

I took down almost the entire middle shelf, rearranged the books into correct order, bottom edge facing me on the desk. They now spelled—with gaps where the books had been replaced out of sequence—ON LY WIN TER IS TRU.

I sat looking at them for a long time. The shock of desecration had subsided. I felt only a wearying sadness.

I returned the books to the bookcase, locked the glass doors and tossed the key away. It landed somewhere under the desk.

After some thought, I retrieved it, and hung it, with the spare, by the clock, in the hall.

HILARY MANTEL

# Winter Break

B Y   T H E   T I M E  they arrived at their destination, they
could no longer recognise their own name. The taxi
driver stabbed the air with his placard while they stood
gawping up and down the line, until Phil pointed and
said: 'That's us.' Little peaks had grown over the 'Ts' in
their surname, and the dot on the 'i' had drifted away
like an island. She rubbed her cheek, numbed by the
draught from the air vent above her seat; the rest of her
felt creased and gritty, and while Phil bustled towards
the man, waving, she picked the cloth of her T-shirt
away from the small of her back, and shuffled after him.
We dress for the weather we want, as if to bully it, even
though we've seen the forecast.

The driver laid a hairy, proprietorial hand on their
baggage trolley. He was a squat man with the regulation
moustache, and he wore a twill zipped jacket with a tartan
lining peeping from under it; as if to say, forget your sunshine illusions. The plane was late and it was already dark.
He flung open a rear door for her and humped their bags
into the back of his estate car. 'Long way,' was all he said.

'Yes, but pre-paid,' Phil said.

The driver plumped down in his seat with a leath-
ery creak. When he slammed his door the whole vehicle

shuddered. The front headrests had been wrenched off, so when he swivelled his body to reverse he threw his arm across both seatbacks and stared past her unseeing, an inch from her face, while she examined his nostril hair by the giddy flash of the car park's lights. 'Sit back, darling,' Phil told her. 'Seatbelt on. Away we go.'

How suited he would have been to fatherhood. Whoops-a-daisy. There, there. No harm done.

But Phil thought otherwise. Always had. He preferred to be able to take a winter break during the school term, when hotel rates were lower. For years now he had passed her newspapers, folded to those reports that tell you how children cost a million pounds before they're 18. 'When you see it set out like that,' he'd say, 'it's frightening. People think they'll get away with hand-me-downs. Half-portions. It doesn't work like that.'

'But our child wouldn't have a drug addiction,' she'd say. 'Not on that scale. It wouldn't be bright enough for Eton. It could go down the road to Hillside Comp. Although, I hear they have head lice.'

'And you wouldn't want to deal with that, would you?' he said: a man laying down his ace.

They inched through the town, the pavements jostling, the cheap bars flashing their signs, and Phil said, as she knew he would, 'I think we made the right decision.' A journey of an hour lay ahead, and they speeded up through the sprawling outskirts; the road began to climb. When she was sure that the driver did not want conversation she eased herself back in her seat. There were two types of taxi man: the garrulous ones with a niece in Dagenham, who wanted to talk right the way out to the far coast and the national park, and the ones who needed every grunt racked out of them, who wouldn't tell you where their niece lived if they were under torture.

She made one or two tourist remarks: how had the weather been? 'Raining. Now I smoke,' the man said. He thrust a cigarette right from the packet into his mouth, juggling a lighter and at one point taking his hands from the wheel entirely. He drove very fast, treating each swerve in the road as a personal insult, fuming at any hold up. She could feel Phil's opinions banking up behind his teeth: now that won't do the gearbox any good, will it? At first, a few cars edged past them, creeping down to the lights of the town. Then the traffic thinned and petered out. As the road narrowed, black and silent hills fell away behind them. Phil began to tell her about the flora and fauna of the high maquis.

She had to imagine the fragrance of herbs crushed underfoot. The car windows were sealed against the still, cool night, and she turned her head deliberately away from her husband and misted the glass with her breath. The fauna was mostly goats. They tumbled down the hill-sides, stones cascading after them, and leapt across the path of the car, kids running at their heels. They were patched and parti-coloured, fleet and heedless. Sometimes an eye gleamed furtive in a headlight. She twitched at the seat-belt, which was sawing into her throat. She closed her eyes.

At Heathrow Phil had been a pain in the security queue. When the young man in front of them bent to pick laboriously at the laces of his hiking boots, Phil said loudly: 'He knows he has to take his shoes off. But he couldn't just have slip-ons, like the rest of us.'

'Phil,' she whispered, 'it's because they're heavy. He wants to wear his boots so they don't count as baggage.'

'I call it selfish. Here's the queue banking up. He knows what's going to happen.'

The hiker glanced up from the tail of his eye. 'Sorry, mate.'

'One day you'll get your head punched in,' she said.

'We'll see, shall we?' Phil said: singing it, like a child in a playground game.

Once, a year or two into their marriage, he had confessed to her that he found the presence of small children unbearably agitating: the unmodulated noise, the strewn plastic toys, the inarticulate demands that you provide something, fix something, though you didn't know what it was.

'On the contrary,' she said. 'They point. They shout, "Juice".'

He nodded miserably. 'A lifetime of that,' he said. 'It would get to you. It would feel like a lifetime.'

Anyway, it was becoming academic now. She had reached that stage in her fertile life when genetic strings got knotted and chromosomes went whizzing around and reattaching themselves. 'Trisomies,' he said. 'Syndromes. Metabolic deficiencies. I wouldn't put you through that.'

She sighed. Rubbed her bare arms. Phil leaned forward. Cleared his throat, spoke to the driver. 'My wife is chilly.'

'Wear the cardigan,' said the driver. He slotted another cigarette into his mouth. The road now ascended in a series of violent bends, and at each of them he wrenched the wheel, throwing the car's back-end out towards the ditches.

'How long?' she asked. 'About?'

'Half-hour.' If he could have concluded the statement by spitting, she felt he would.

'Still in time for dinner,' Phil said encouragingly. He rubbed her arms for her, as if to give encouragement. She laughed shakily. 'You make them wobble,' she said.

'Nonsense. There's no flesh on you.'

There was a cloudy half-moon, a long scoop of fallen land to their right, a bristling treeline above them, and as he cupped her elbow, caressing it, there was once more a skid and slide, a rock-shower rattling inconsequentially to the road before them. Phil was just saying: 'It'll only take me two minutes to unpack.' He was beginning to explain to her his system for travelling light. But the driver grunted, wrenched the wheel, stabbed the brakes and brought them lurching to a halt. She shot forward, jarring her wrist on the seat in front. The seatbelt pulled her back. They had felt the impact but seen nothing. The driver swung open his door and ducked out into the night. 'Kid,' Phil whispered.

Gone under? The driver was pulling something from between the front wheels. He was bent double and they could see his bottom rise in the air, with the frill of tartan at his waist. Inside the body of the car they sat very still, as if not to draw attention to the incident. They did not look at each other, but watched as the driver straightened up, rubbed the small of his back, then walked around and lifted the tailgate, pulling out something dark, like a tarpaulin. The chill of the night hit them between their shoulder blades, and fractionally they shrank together. Phil took her hand. She twitched it away: not petulant, but because she felt she needed to concentrate. The driver appeared in silhouette before them, lit by their own head-lights. He turned his head and glanced up and down the empty road. He had something in his hand, a rock. He stooped. Thud, thud, thud. She tensed. She wanted to cry out. Thud, thud, thud. The man straightened up. There was a bundle in his arms. Tomorrow's dinner, she thought. Seethed in onion and tomato sauce. She didn't know why the word 'seethed' came to her. She remembered a sign down in the town: The Sophocles School of Motoring. 'Call no man happy . . .' The driver posted the bundle into the back of the car, by their luggage. The tailgate slammed.

Recycling, she thought. Phil would say 'Very laudable'. If he spoke. But it seemed he had decided not to. She understood that they wouldn't, either of them, mention this dire start to their winter break. She cradled her wrist. Gently, gently. A movement of anxiety. A washing. Massaging the minute pain away. I shall go on hearing it, she thought, at least for the rest of this week: thud, thud, thud. We might make a joke of it, perhaps. How we froze. How we let him get on with it, what else could we . . . because you don't get vets patrolling the mountains by night. Something rose into her throat, that she wanted to articulate: tickled her hard palate, fell away again.

The porter said: 'Welcome to the Royal Athena Sun.' Light spilled from a marble interior, and near at hand some cold broken columns were spot-lit, the light shifting from blue to green and back again. That will be the 'archaeological feature' as promised, she thought. Another time she would have grinned at the exuberant vulgarity. But the clammy air, the incident . . . she inched out of the car and straightened up, unsmiling, her hand resting on the taxi's roof. The driver nudged past her without a word. He lifted the tailgate. But the porter, hovering helpful, was behind him. He reached for their bags with both hands. The driver moved swiftly, blocking him, and to her own amazement she jumped forward, 'No!' and so did Phil, 'No!'

'I mean,' Phil said. 'It's only two bags.' As if to prove the lightness of the load, he had gripped one of the bags in his own fist, and he gave it a joyous twirl. 'I believe in —'

he said. But the phrase 'travelling light' eluded him. 'Not much stuff,' he said.

'Okay, sir.' The porter shrugged. Stepped back. She rehearsed it in her mind, as if telling it to a friend, much later: you see, we were made complicit. But the taxi driver didn't do anything wrong, of course. Just something efficient.

And her imaginary friend agreed: still, instinctively you would feel, you would feel there was something to hide.

'I'm ready for a drink,' Phil said. He was yearning for the scene beyond the plate glass: brandy sours, clanking ice-cubes in the shape of fish, clicking high heels on terracotta tiles, wrought iron scrollwork, hotel linen, soft pillow. Call no man happy. Call no man happy until he has gone down to his grave in peace. Or at least to his junior suite: and can rub out today and wake tomorrow hungry. The taxi driver leaned into the car to scoop out the second bag. As he did, he nudged aside the tarpaulin, and what she glimpsed—and in the same moment, refused to see—was not a cloven hoof, but the grubby hand of a human child.

LEE ROURKE

# Emergency Exit

Y OU'RE SITTING AT your desk as usual. Staring at the spreadsheet displayed on the flat-screen monitor positioned ergonomically in front of you. As according to company policy, the screen is perfectly aligned with your line of vision. There's nothing that should cause you any discomfort or disturb your tasks at hand. Yet, you still feel unsettled by something. Nothing of any interest is happening around you. There are, for instance, no sudden breakdowns, mental or electronic, to keep you amused. There's no idle gossip for you to tune into at your leisure, filtering through to your finely tuned ear over the partition that separates one team from another, just the endless assault of clicks, shuffling and hard-drives whirring into motion. You get up from your seat and move away from your desk. Your colleagues are oblivious to your movements. You walk backwards, at an angle that is diagonal from your desk, towards the gap that leads to the walkway.

On the walk-way you pass the filing cabinets, walking forwards now, glancing at your colleagues to your immediate left. They remain motionless, glued—just like you were — to their monitors, fingers tapping across their wireless keyboards.

You hardly know what you're doing. You don't care what you're doing. You head towards the door to the company kitchen; all in all it's about 15 metres from your desk. It's a walk you complete, back and forth, about 30 maybe 40 times per day. The air-conditioning unit hums above you. You can hear it now, away from your desk. The air is thick with heat and it seems to you that the air-conditioning unit is struggling to cope. Nevertheless, you are breathing normally, though you're a little sticky around your neck and lower back. This doesn't bother you, though. You open the door to the kitchen. It's empty. You can smell the cheap coffee the company provides brewing in the two percolators to your left. Again, you walk diagonally across the room, to your right, towards a door. Above the door a sign reads:

EMERGENCY EXIT

The door is locked. You stand there for a moment, staring at the sign above your head. You notice its font—possibly Helvetica or maybe Microsoft Sans Serif. It elicits no reaction from you whatsoever, in keeping with its design. A sign of this nature must never cause any alarm, you think. It must simply and calmly direct those who seek its guidance towards safety. After 12.3 seconds you divert your eyes down towards the lock. In emergencies you understand that to open the door you must smash the glass cylinder keeping the spring-action bolt—which acts as the door's lock—firmly in place. You immediately look for something to smash the glass cylinder with. Attached to the lock is a small cosh on a chain. You quickly smash the cylinder with it. The bolt springs back with considerable force, disappearing into the doorframe as the shards of glass fall to the floor by your shoes. Without looking back, you open the door.

You walk onto the stairwell. You're on the eighth floor. You momentarily consider walking up the two floors to the roof, but you don't, you walk slowly, calmly downwards — not really knowing why. The stairs are empty and the echo of your feet hitting each step can be heard. You turn right onto the seventh floor, and then the sixth, spiralling downwards towards the ground floor. When you reach the landing of the fourth floor you suddenly stop.

There's a man standing there.

He's motionless and looks like he's been standing there for a very long time. You look at him. He's wearing a suit. He's holding his briefcase to his chest. He looks terrified. Fear has completely taken hold of him, you think. He's stiff with terror. You look at him. His eyes stare straight ahead. His face is trembling, ever so slightly. It's only noticeable once you lean in towards him. There are small beads of sweat on his forehead.

You stare at him.

You move closer to him, half expecting him to move, or to run away, but he doesn't. He continues to stare straight ahead, not through you, but past you. You must know I'm here, you think. You must be able to see me? You stare at him. He continues to stare straight ahead, his eyes darting past you, towards the wall behind your back. You stare at him. Come on, you think, what's wrong with you? Say something! Say something! He stares straight ahead. You look at him. You decide to say something.

'What are you doing?' you say.

He stares straight ahead, past you, towards the wall behind you, the white, nondescript wall. His eyes fixed.

'What are you doing?' you continue.

27

He stares straight ahead. You inch closer to him. Surely you can feel my breath now? you think. He lifts his hand to his mouth, dropping his briefcase to the floor. He looks like he's smoking an imaginary cigarette. His expression changes and now he has a vacant gaze, like absolutely nothing is happening within him, like nothing can touch him. His hand slowly falls back down to his side. He takes a deep breath and exhales, slowly, his shoulders relaxing. You look at him, but still he doesn't look at you. He looks past you, like he's looking at something more interesting over your shoulder, something on the nondescript white wall. You feel empty. You feel like you don't exist. You feel like nothing exists. Finally, you feel nothing. Then he lifts his hand to his mouth again. Exactly like he did a moment ago, you think. Maybe a little more slowly this time. He calmly lets his hand fall back down by his side. Again he takes a deep breath and exhales, slowly, like he's trying to expend as little energy as possible. You look at him, but he doesn't seem to notice you doing this. You don't know what to do. You've never been in a situation quite like this before. You feel uncomfortable. You can't stand still. You begin to shuffle. You begin to itch. You begin to feel agitated. You don't know what to do. You decide to say something.

'What are you doing?' you ask.

He stares straight ahead. His eyes fixed, looking straight past you.

'What are you doing?' you continue.

He stares straight ahead. You want to shake him. To strike out. You want to kick him in the shins. Knee him where it hurts. You want to wake him up from his torpor. You want to know what it is he's doing. You want to know why he's standing there, on the stairs, on the fourth floor, on the landing . . . in the company stairwell. You want to know how long he's been standing there.

'How long have you been standing there?' you ask.

He stares straight ahead. Then he lifts his hand to his mouth again, before letting it fall slowly back down by his side. Quite calmly he breaths in and out, without a care in the world, you think. You look at his eyes: they're large and blank—like they're seeing nothing. Like two black dots have been painted on his face. Everything, you think, is without meaning or consequence. He doesn't blink. He just stares past you, away from you, over your shoulder. You don't know what to do or say. You decide to say something anyway.

'Please tell me why you're here?' you say.

He stares straight ahead. The wall behind him, like the wall behind you, is white. He stands before it, cutting his image across it. Like a silhouette, you think. He lifts one of his hands. He lifts it towards his head. Then he lifts his other hand. He lifts it towards his head. He slowly scratches his head and then lets both hands fall slowly back by his side.

You look at him.

He looks at you; a sideways glance.

Then he decides to say something to you.

'I don't know why I am here,' he says.

He turns to stare at you. He stares at you.

'Where are you going?' he asks.

You stare at him. He stares at you. You look into his eyes—two dark pools of nothingness. Everything, you think, is without consequence and meaningless. His hands are by his side. He isn't moving. You decide to say something to him.

'I don't know where I'm going,' you say.

He stares straight ahead, away from you, behind you,

over your shoulder. He lifts his hand to his mouth. Like he's smoking an imaginary cigarette, you think. You look at him as his hand falls slowly back down by his side. He stares straight ahead. You look away. You look away at the stairs leading down to the third floor. You walk away. You walk down the stairs. Down. Down towards the third floor. Away from him. You leave him standing there. You walk away. Down.

You don't look back.

You can't look back.

You walk away.

Down.

LEONE ROSS

# Love Silk Food

M RS NEECY BROWN'S husband is falling in love. She can tell because the love is stuck to the walls of house, making the wallpaper sticky, and it seeps into the calendar in her kitchen, so bad that she can't see what the date is and the love keeps ruining the food: whatever she does or however hard she concentrates, everything turns to mush. The dumplings lack squelch and bite — they come out doughy and stupid, like grey belches floating in her carefully salted water. Her famed liver and green banana is mush too: everything has become too soft and falling apart, like food made for babies. Silk food, her mother used to call it.

Mrs Neecy Brown's husband is falling in love. Not with her, no.

She gets away from the love in the walls by visiting Wood Green Shopping City on a Saturday afternoon. She sits in the foyer on a bench for nearly two hours, between Evans and Shoe Mart. She doesn't like the shoes there: the heels make too much noise, and why are the clothes that Evans make for heavy ladies always sleeveless? No decorum, she thinks, all that flesh out-of-doors. She likes that word. It sounds like a lady's word, and it suits her just fine.

There are three days left to Christmas and the ceiling is a forest of cheap gold tinsel and dusty red cartridge paper. People walk past in fake fur hoods and boots; a woman stands by the escalator, her hand slipped into the front of her coat; she seems calm but she also looks like she's holding her heart, below the fat tartan-print scarf around her neck. Then Mrs Neecy Brown sees that the woman by the escalator is her and that she's standing outside her own skin looking at herself, something her granny in Jamaica taught her to do when the world don't feel right. People are staring, so she slips back inside her body and heads home, past a man pushing a flat-faced mop across the mall floor like he's taking it for a walk.

She trudges through Saturday crowds that are smelly and noisy. The young people have fat bottom lips and won't pick up their feet, and she has a moment of pride, thinking of *her* girls. Normal teenagers they were, with their moods, but one word from she or one face-twist from Mr Brown, and there was a stop to that! She had all six daughters between 1961 and 1970: a cube, a three-dimensional heptagon, a rectangle that came out just bigger than the size of her fist and the triangles, oh! The two of them so prickly that she locked up shop on Mr Brown for nearly seven months. He was so careful when he finally got back in that their last daughter was a perfectly satisfactory and smooth-sided sphere.

All grown now, scattered across north London, descending on the house every Sunday and also other days in the week, looking for babysitting; pardner-throwing; domino games; approval; advice about underwear and aerated water; argument; looking for Mamma's rub-belly hand during that time of the month; to curse men and girlfriends; to leave pets even though she never liked animals in the house; to talk in striated, incorrect patois and hug-up with their Daddy. Then Melba, the sphere, who had grown even rounder in adulthood, came to live upstairs with her baby's father and their two children. The three-year-old sucked the sofa so much he swallowed all the pink off the right-hand cushions. The eight-month-old had inherited his father's mosquito face and long limbs and delicate stomach which meant everyone had to wade through baby sick, and Lara, Melba's best friend from middle school, arrived in a bomber jacket with a newly pierced and bleeding lip so many years ago that Mrs Neecy Brown didn't even remember when but regarded her with fond absent-mindedness, not unlike a decoration you've had so long you don't know where it came from. And the noise. Oh dear, oh Lord.

In between all of this, her husband's bouts of lovesick-ness.

He'd proved no good at marriage: the repetition, the crying babies, the same good mornings, the per-fectly decent nightdresses she bought—*Lord, woman, you couldn't try a little harder*—but there was nothing wrong with the pretty Marks and Spencer cotton shifts, lace at the décolletage, and little cream and brown flowers and yellow and red flowers. Just that he craved what she called the Excitement Girls. She thought of them as wet things: oiled spines, sweating lips, damp laps. She saw one of them once, kissing him goodbye no more than fifteen minutes from their home, and she'd scuttled behind a stone pillar and peeped. The girl turned away after the kiss. She looked happy. Her chest was jiggling, bra-less, the nipples like bullets.

*That's what they look like then*, thought Mrs Neecy Brown.

❧

She paused at the entrance to Wood Green tube station. One turn to the left and she'd be on her street. No, she wouldn't go home, not yet. For he'd be there for his tea, pirouetting through the house with all his broad grins and smacking her bottom, his voice too loud. When he's in love he's alternately lascivious and servile and too easily excited into anything: brawls, TV shows, games of poker for too much money. Gone too long and out too often and when he comes back he lunges at the family: *Come, let's go to Chessington Park next Sunday—or we could—or we could*—and he gets all his grandchildren excited, and she fries chicken and makes potato salad and buys Sainsbury's sausage rolls, 39 pence the packet of ten, and packs tomatoes like a proper English family does, in a proper hamper basket and thermoses of tea. How stupid he thought she was, didn't he know she could *see*, that she knew him? And then when all is ready, the greatest of apologies he comes to them with. Once he even squeezed out tears: *Can't come, Mrs Brown*, he calls her, or Mummy on affectionate days, *Can't come, my dears. They working me like a bitch dog, you know* and *Errol*, she murmurs, *language, Errol*. Then he's heading out the house, tripping up on his own sunshine, radiating free, free. *Make sure you come back in time, Errol boy*, she would think, *in time to wash that woman's nipples off your neck-back*.

After all.

She loves the London underground; it still seems a treat, an adventure, paying your fare, riding the escalator, choosing a seat, settling back to watch the people. So many different kinds of people, from all over the world! Today's no different. She settles herself into a corner and watches a Chinese boy struggling with a huge backpack. The straps are caught in his long hair. She'll ride with him all the way to Heathrow, she thinks. See if he untangles the hair before Green Park. Then ride the way back. She leans her head on the glass partition and steps outside of her body.

Last night he'd done something he'd never done in all the years of his lying, stinking cheating.

Walking in, about midnight or thereabouts, easing himself onto the edge of the mattress, she pretending to be asleep as usual, groaned a little, turned on her side. And he rolled into the bed, after casting one shoe hither and the other thither and his tongue was in her ear digging and rooting. Snuffle, snuffle, like a pig, she thought. Then she became aware of the smells. Vicks VapoRub. Someone else's perfume, and . . . Mrs Neecy Brown lay trembling and affronted and frozen in the first alarm and rage she'd let herself feel for a long time, not since the first time he cheated, and repented and wept so much and talked to pastor for weeks and then just went out and did it again and she'd realised that it was a habit, this love-falling, and that she could never stop it, only fold her own self into a little twist of paper and stuff herself near the mops and brooms in the downstairs cupboard, no not since then had she let herself cry. He'd come to her bed unwashed, with the smell of another woman's underneath on him, all over him.

She felt as if her head was rising: she would never have guessed that she could recognise such an odour, that she would so accurately know it when it assailed her. But it was just like the smell of her own underneath, the one that she made sure to clean and dress, like a gleaming, newly caught fish, lest it flop from between her thighs and swim upriver.

She clapped a hand over her mouth as he snuggled into her, so she didn't leap up and scream it at him: *Is so all woman underneath smell the same, Errol?*

35

If they were all the same, why turn from her and seek another?

Let him eat what bits he could find in the fridge for tea, and vex with her, and use it as an excuse to go on bad and storm off to *she*.

She looks at her company. The Chinese boy has sagged next to the centre pole, holding on for dear life. There are many empty seats, but perhaps getting the mammoth backpack on and off is so hard that he's decided to stand all the way. There's another young man sitting to her right. He's wearing a blue shirt and navy blue pants. His black socks are covered in fluff, like a carpet that hasn't been Hoovered in days. He has a dry, occasional cough and he sits with one hand akimbo, the other on his jaw. His eyes dart around. He needs a good woman if she's ever seen one. She looks closer, sees she's wrong—someone has creamed his skin and it gleams amongst the imperfection.

Furthest away are a mother and daughter, stamps of each other, but even if they hadn't been, she would have known. Mothers and daughters sit together in particular ways. Mother is shorter, more vibrant. She rubs her temples, manipulating her whole face like it's ginger dough. Daughter has a face like a steamed pudding, two plaits that begin above her ears and slop straight down over them. Her hand's a wedge of flesh, rubbing her eye. She smiles at Mrs Neecy Brown, who finds she can't smile back. She can't take the chance. She presumes that Mr Brown finds his girls in north London; he's lazy. This latest one is near, she can feel it; she could even be this young woman. She wonders whether they know her face, if they've ever followed her.

The train stops, empties, fills, whizzes past stations: Turnpike Lane, Manor House, Finsbury Park, Arsenal,

Holloway Road? Where was she, this latest, casually breaking off bits of her husband and keeping them for herself? She'd had to feed breakfast to a limbless man at least twice; can't forget the week he didn't smile at all because some selfish woman had stolen his lips.

She doesn't realise that she's asleep until she wakes up.
  'Sis?'
  Balding head and a large beauty mark on his left jowl. He hunches forward in the seat; he's been sitting like that for years, she knows the type, bad habits you couldn't break by the time the fifties set in. There's something young about his chin: it's smooth and plump and might quiver when he cries. He's wearing a horrible, mustard-yellow jacket and red trousers.
  The man is bending forward, gesticulating, and Mrs Neecy Brown sees that her scarf has fallen to the floor. She leans forward at the waist, feeling creaky, bleary, feeling her breasts hang, glimmers at the man who's smiling to her and beats her to it, scoops up the scarf and places it delicately on her knee, like a present.
  'Thank you.'
  'You welcome.'
  She looks around; they've reached Heathrow. She's been asleep for an hour, at least! The train hisses. People come slowly. They'll be heading back soon. She looks out at them. She'd like to be a movie star, to pack her trousseau in a perfect set of matching luggage and leave the house, and the sky would be full of a crescent, golden moon above her. She would come to Heathrow and . . . what? She sighs. The fantasy won't hold. She doesn't have a good suitcase any more, because triangle number one borrowed it and still hasn't given it back and she knows what that means. Last time she asked for it, she brought

her heavy-duty black garbage bags from Sainsbury's, where she works.

The train jerks and the scarf jolts forward again and spews onto the floor. The man picks it up again, before she can move.

'Look like that scarf don't want to stay with you.'

Sudden rage floods her.

'What you know about me or anything? Mind you bloody business.'

'Oh my,' says the man. He touches a hand to his forehead. 'I'm very sorry, lady.' His voice is slow and somewhat wet, like a leaf in the autumn. A crushed, gleaming-wet leaf, in shades of gold and red and yellow.

She grunts: an apology of sorts. He recognises the timbre, inclines his head.

She thinks of her girls. If any of them is a cheater, it's the second triangle, one vaguely cast eye and a pretty pair of legs. Never could stop needing attention. She sighs. Anger will help nothing.

'You alright, sis?' The autumn man looks concerned.

'What business of yours?'

'Just . . .' he gestures. 'You look like something important on you mind.'

'Nobody don't tell you that you mustn't talk to strangers on the Underground?'

He hoots. 'That is the rule? Well, them tell me England people shy.'

Silence. He has a suitcase. Marked and scrawled. She remembers arriving in London, so long ago, and how it seemed everything was in boxes: the houses, the gardens, the children, and how big and cold the air was and that everything seemed inter-cut with red: double-decker buses and phone boxes and lipstick. Mounds of dog doo on the street and how you could smoke in public places.

She, a youngish bride, Errol like a cock, waving his large behind and his rock-hard stomach, he'd kicked up dirt in the back yard that he would eventually make her garden, and crowed at the neighbours. Mrs Smith from two doors down came to see what the noise was and she brought a home-made trifle and she was always in and out after that, helping with the girls, her blonde, cotton-wool head juddering in heartfelt kindness. She'd needed Mrs Smith.

'So you come from Jamaica?'

'St Elizabeth. Real country.'

'Where you headed?'

The man consulted a slip of paper from his lapel pocket. '32 Bruce Grove, Wood Green.'

'Well, that's just near where I am, I can show you.'

They regard each other for some seconds.

'You come to —?'

'You live with —?'

Laughing, and the softening of throats and her hands dance at her neck, tying up the scarf. He has a grin perched on the left hand side of his face.

'Ladies first,' he says.

'You come to see family for Christmas?'

He nods. 'My daughter married an English husband and her child is English. So I come to see them, first time.' He seems to let himself and his excitement loose, slapping his hands on his thighs and humming. 'Yes, boy, my first grandchild.'

She smiles. 'I know you have a picture.'

He scrabbles in his wallet and passes it over. His daughter is dark black and big-boned and big-haired, the husband tall and beaming, the child surprisingly anaemic and small-eyed. She has a snotty nose. Mrs Neecy Brown thinks that an English person must have taken the photograph, for anyone she knows better would have wiped it.

But they look very happy. Grubby but happy, Mrs Smith would have said. Dead now a year or so, she was. She hands the picture back.

'Pretty.'

He nods vigorously, slaps his thighs again, stows the photo carefully back inside the dreadful coat, blows on his clenched fists. He must be cold, she thinks.

Night lies down on Wood Green station as they puff their way out and stand, gazing at the road. My, how they've talked! Not easy at all; she can't remember the last time she talked to a man who was listening. The sound of her voice was like a tin, she thought, rattling money. But he opened his mouth and made sounds, and so did she, all the way home. The smell of vinegar and chips from a nearby shop, three boys play-wrestling in front of the cinema across the road: some wag had called it Hollywood Green. She doesn't know whether she thinks it's clever or stupid. She points.

'What you think of that name?'

He reads, shakes his head. He doesn't have an opinion. She smiles. That's just fine, with her.

A cat tromps by, meowing. Lord, the noise. Mrs Neecy Brown drops her handbag and grabs the autumn man's arm, and reaches up to his shoulder, fingers scrabbling, her wedding ring golden against his terrible jacket. She hates cats. They don't seem to care.

He puts his suitcase down and pats her hand. They stand like that, arms interlinked, her hand on his shoulder, his hand patting. She is aware of happiness. The smell of vinegar, the scattered cigarette butts.

Eventually she moves away and he picks up the suit-case. Her fingers tingle from the shape of his shoulder. She waves towards the darkened roads. 'I show you where.'

There's mist between them when they find number 32, mist where he's breathing from carrying the suitcase. She can see fairy lights in the window of the house and hear the sound of Slade's 'Merry Xmas Everybody' coming from somewhere.

The autumn man rifles in his suitcase. He holds something out to her.

'Some of my wife Christmas cake. She make a good cake, rich. You will like it.'

The tips of her fingers explode as she touches the foil paper. She's aware that her mouth is slightly open. Wife, well. Of course, wife. He is a big man.

'I must be going now,' she says.

He smiles at her, she smiles back, at this orange man standing in front of a dull wall. A light has come on in the front room; perhaps they've been watching for him.

'Daddy!'

The young woman flings herself forward and he hugs her close.

'Andy, bring Precious! Bring her! Oh no, don't bring her, cold out here. Andy, don't bring her, you hear? We coming in! Come, daddy!'

Then she sees Mrs Neecy Brown.

'Good evening?' she says. The vowels have slowed and lengthened.

'Good evening,' says Mrs Neecy Brown. There is something moving up and down her back, some unknown discomfort. What is it? The husband has come out of the house now, thinner and better looking than his photograph, and he's disobeyed his wife, has a shy child on his hip and the autumn man who has a wife, of course he does, is tousling the child's plaits and the men are pumping hands. *I don't know his name*, thinks Mrs Neecy Brown. She feels absurdly forgotten. Shuffles. The daughter is like a piece of tall, sharp glass. She has thrust the moonlight in the front yard between them.

Oh, glaring.

'Well . . .' says Mrs Neecy Brown. She shivers; she has the wrong coat on, she thinks. Too thin for this time of the year.

'Well?' says the daughter. The suggestion in her tone is unmistakeable. Move from my yard and my father, you woman. You Excitement Girl.

She wants to laugh. Could she be that dangerous? Could she be that pulsing sun?

'I — no, no —' she struggles. She tries again. 'You—I—'

'Goodnight, goodnight,' calls the autumn man, who doesn't know her name either and gleams less now. That absence of names might have been romantic in a movie, but suddenly Mrs Neecy Brown sees it all as the daughter does: sordid, undignified. Shamed, she lifts her hand to wave, so that it will be finished, but the men have already turned their backs, heading inside, making the sounds of cockerels at each other, the formerly shy child trilling *Granddaddy, granddaddy*! They are gone.

The daughter growls, like an angry cat.

Mrs Neecy Brown draws herself up and flattens her stomach against her backbone. For after all. What a presumption.

The daughter growls again.

Mrs Neecy Brown lifts her face.

'I am a good woman,' she says, calmly.

The house door clicks shut.

There are Christmas lights and gleaming trees in people's front rooms. She walks slowly, savouring the cold whipping her shoulders. Under the streetlight you can see she's eating another woman's Christmas cake, licking the black rum-soaked softness off her tingling fingers, like silk food, her mother used to say.

# Feather Girls

'YOU HAVE TO catch their coats whilst they're young.' That was the saying he'd been brought up with, in a village full of thin, white-haired women who saw nothing wrong in telling their sons how best to trap a girl, as they themselves had once been trapped.

The sun sparkled on the peat-coloured lake below, making magic of dun. He took his time on the long road down to the village. Avoided pot holes and sheep muck and loose chips of stone tumbled from the walls. Midges rolled in clouds overhead. He tugged at the long grass that sprouted at the roadside and bent it, twisted it, threaded it through his fingers, snapped it. All these years of going to meet her and yet still, every time, he felt like a lad. His stomach might as well be in a boat out on the lake.

The sign outside the Hare and Anchor was cracked, and the paint so faded you could barely make out the image of a brown hare, its ears wrapped around a silver anchor. It was a locals' pub, sandwiched between crumbling cottages with mildewed net curtains, further up the steep hill than outsiders cared to venture. Tourists were catered for beside the lake, where they swarmed off ferries into gift shops and outdoor clothing shops and took cream tea in cafes where the lacy nets were clean. She would pass all that on her way up the hill. Had she left the lake already? Crossed the narrow shingle beach, stepped on to the pavement, webbed feet becoming toes, dripping feather coat hung over what was her wing but now an arm.

'Usual, Bill?' Mary, the landlady, put aside the television listings magazine she'd been reading.

'And a glass of tap water and a—'

'Packet of salt and vinegar crisps. Meeting her tonight, are you, love?'

He didn't reply, just waited for his pint of mild to be drawn and watched the empty table by the fireplace.

'You know,' said Mary, 'you should have caught her coat whilst she was young.'

A collection of regulars cluttered the bar, all greyhaired men a similar age to him. He knew many of them had caught themselves feather girls. On summer evenings when they were lads they would gather beside the lake and try to gain favour by lobbing in the biggest pieces of bread. Home baked worked best. His cousin Johnny had walloped a whole loaf in once but that had backfired when a greedy girl near choked on it. He married her though. Eileen she took as her name.

He handed Mary the exact change and carried the drinks and crisps over to the table. It wasn't like her to be late. He placed the glasses on the already sodden beer mats and shook a dribble of mild from his fingers. The fire wasn't lit. Mary was stingy with the coal, still too early in the year for a fire whatever the chill in the air said.

Collections of one kind or another littered the pub, whisky boxes, empty wine bottles, framed pictures of 1930s film stars who would never have visited a place like this. There were three dart boards on one wall, but nobody remembered where the darts were. On the mantelpiece there were stacks of glass ash trays, scorched and lined with grit. A monument to times past, or testament to the fact Mary could never throw anything away.

He hadn't heard her come in but there she was. The pale skin of her cheeks looked damp, her dark eyes nervous. She was tall and slight in her downy white under dress, and she compulsively twiddled her fingers, as though when she had them she couldn't bear not to be using them. She tucked her feather coat beneath the table and perched on a stool. He shifted his legs back so he wouldn't have to know the feathers were there, brushing against his trousers.

He opened the crisps, split the foil of the packet and pulled it apart so they could share.

Delicate lines appeared around her eyes and mouth as she smiled. She tried to speak but her voice was too hoarse; she dipped her head.

He nodded. It always took a while for the words to come out right, for her to find her human voice. He didn't have that excuse.

She plucked at the crisps with her fingers. He always found this movement intriguing to watch; it was as though her fingers became her beak and her long thin arm took the place of her graceful neck.

As they found their voices they talked of the lake, the speed of the boats, the damaged reed beds, squabbles with her neighbours, unruly coots and forever diving cormorants, the quality of the waterwort, the spread of swamp stonecrop.

'I'll take these for you, shall I?' Mary intruded, fingers already grasping the not quite empty glasses. 'I'll bring you some more, and another packet of them crisps too.'

She nodded. She wouldn't speak to Mary, or to anyone else but him as far as he'd ever seen.

His Grandmother had been a feather girl, strict and cold. She'd never found where his grandfather had hidden her coat. He'd heard people from elsewhere tell other tales about white feathers; if you found one it meant an angel had visited, or there were rumours about young girls giving them to men in civvies during the war to show them up as cowards. In the village a found feather meant one of the girls was itching to fly away. They sometimes grew back in the crook of an elbow or at the back of the neck, but they soon fell out. He had found one of his Grandmother's in the bread bin once. Stuffed it in his pocket, then kept it for weeks tucked between the pages of a precious *Dandy*. Finally he'd set it out to sail on the lake, on a December day as the cloudy surface was beaten with rain.

His wife came from the south. She'd had no time for the 'silly swan stories', said the abundance of white-haired women in the village was down to inbreeding. She'd said a lot else as well. She'd flown off herself as soon as the children were grown.

Mary plonked the glasses down. Foam and water coursed from the soggy mats and pooled on the table. Mary waited for a moment, but soon gave up and stalked back to the bar.

He split the packet, as before. The tips of her fingers touched his knuckles as they both reached for a crisp. He pulled away.

He already knew how the evening would go. How the dusk would settle outside as they talked in hushed voices. How, when they had sat for too long with the empty glasses and the empty crisp packet between them they would know it was time to go. She would clutch her feather coat and they would say a quick goodbye on the doorstep of the pub, between the abandoned hanging

47

baskets. He would try not to watch her walk down the road towards the lights that twinkled on the water at the edge of the lake. He would try not to worry about the chill in the air and her shivering because she would not put her feather coat back on until she'd reached the water. He would try not to linger on the buckled moorland road, watched by his stern-faced sheep, their coats grey in the twilight. He would try not to hear his plodding footsteps matched by the sound of wings beating overhead as he made his way towards the squat stone building that was home.

For now, he would watch her fingers peck at the last crumbs in the crisp packet, and listen to the collection of voices drone beside the bar, and the clink of glasses as Mary pretended to tidy up.

## CHRISTOPHER BURNS

# Foreigner

WHEN I RETURNED it was to a celebration fit for heroes. Banners had been hoisted across buildings, flags draped from windows, and a proud and happy country greeted every homecoming. The woman I would marry had waited for hours on a thronged quayside, and when we met we clung together so tightly that it seemed our very bones were interlinked.

All that was a long time ago and it doesn't always happen that way. Sometimes it's different. Sometimes we are escorted down a respectfully muffled street. Flags are lowered in salute and mute tearful women throw single roses onto shiny black hearses.

Today I have to wait in freezing drizzle until the front door is unlocked, and then my wife and I stand looking at each other for a few seconds. My hands are pushed deep into the pockets of my combat trousers as if searching for the keys I once owned. I tell myself that I'm almost as cold as I was on that trek across the island. It would only irritate Debbie if I admit this, so I just apologise for being late.

'Is this deliberate?' she asks.

'No,' I insist. A fabricated excuse dies in my throat because I know that she will see straight through it. It takes a few seconds before she responds.

'All right,' she says, 'but I want you out of here in thirty minutes. We have just enough time.'

I nod understandingly but I know she'll recognise my disdain. 'Of course. Vince.'

'That's right,' she answers crisply, 'Vince.'

Maybe because I haven't seen the new man in her life I am often troubled by curiosity and envy.

'Come on then,' she says. 'We'll get you sorted.'

Debbie opens the door further and I step inside. The house looks and smells different, and at the bottom of the stairs there's a shaded rectangle on the wallpaper where my photograph had once hung. I take off my cap and hang my coat on a hook inside the door as though I still had ownership. Increasingly I feel like an invader in what had once been my home.

'You've let your hair grow a bit too long this time,' Debbie says. 'You haven't shaved either, and you don't suit stubble. When was it last cut?'

'You did it a while back. Just before we got the news.'

She nods quickly. 'I remember.'

I wonder if I should grimace or shrug or reach out my hand or perhaps even embrace her, but while I am pondering she walks quickly into the living room and I follow like an obedient dog.

A new portrait of Alex has appeared amongst the five others on the small table at one side of the room. A photograph of our wedding, and one of me receiving my medal, had stood there once. I wonder what Debbie has done with them—put them in a suitcase under the bed, probably. She makes all her own decisions now. She's independent. My opinion is like my past—it means nothing.

Near the far window, where the light is stronger, there's a straight-backed chair. The hairdressing clippers, scissors, and comb have been placed on the table beside it. If I wanted, I could sit there and watch the home-recorded DVD playing on the television. Men in helmets and desert camouflage are crouched behind a rough mud-brick wall. Spiky palms sprout on the far side of the wall. Gunfire crackles in the slightly unreal way that it sounds on a recording, as if a shot could cause but little harm.

'You're watching him again.'

'I can't stop,' Debbie admits. 'Anyway, I know you do the same. Do you want me to switch it off before he turns?'

'That would be wrong, wouldn't it—a kind of insult.'

She picks up the remote in readiness.

After a few seconds Alex turns his head. I know that he is in part-profile for about the length of a slow intake of breath, and before he can turn aside Debbie pauses the recording. Alex is young, handsome, determined, and professional. With all motion frozen like that he seems like a man with a whole life ahead.

'He looks just like you used to look,' she says.

'A long time ago.'

'Yes,' she agrees, 'a long time ago.'

Debbie presses the play button again. Alex turns his face away from us and the noise of shooting resumes. She presses the off buttons. The screen goes a lifeless grey.

'Take a seat,' she instructs me, her briskness emphasising that we don't have much time. Certainly she wants me out of the way before Vince arrives.

As soon as I sit down she places a towel across my shoulders. The scissors click behind my ear as if being tested for sharpness. I remember how I was told in training that scissors jabbed with the right force in the right place could kill within seconds. At the same time I was also shown how to throttle someone with a metal hair-dressing comb.

The outer edge of a blade slides across the back of my neck. I have heard men killed with bayonets and will never forget the sound.

'You'll not make me look stupid, will you?'

'I've only been cutting hair for thirty years. Look, it makes things difficult if you move. I don't *need* to do this, you know.'

'Why do it, then?'

'Because *someone* has to take care of you, that's why. You'd look like a tramp if you had your own way. What woman would think twice about you when you look like this? You're still a good-looking man, you know. Sort of. I remember when you were younger and spruced up you were really attractive. No wonder I fancied you.'

Debbie is concentrating so hard that her sentences are broken by pauses.

'And besides,' she says, 'I have to get on with the everyday things in life. So do you. That's important. That's what they tell you to do. Otherwise you'll just . . . go under.'

To steady my head she spreads her fingers firmly across my skull. I can feel their pressure. A curl of hair falls on my sleeve. It's lank and streaked with grey.

'Hold *still*. Yes, you used to be really handsome.'

'I was a different person back then.'

'We both were. Things came between us.'

'I was never unfaithful. Never.'

'Don't be stupid. I mean the wars. Your war. Alex's war. Except that they weren't your wars. Not really. They were someone else's.'

And I think again of the dead soldier stretched out on the wintry hill a cold dark ocean away. His bare head was tilted back and his unshaven jaw was thrust upwards so that each separate bristle showed dark and clear above his startlingly white throat. His left arm was crooked beside him, the other lay across his chest with its fingers grasping something within his uniform. Away in the distance a chill noiseless dawn had broken across bare hills stripped of colour.

'Whether they're our wars or someone else's, they're still worth fighting,' I insist.

The scissors pause. 'How can you say that? How can you even think it, when you lost friends and now you've lost your son?'

'Because it's the only way to make sense of things. You've got to believe in what you're doing. When we landed—'

'For God's sake, *please* don't give me another lecture on the past.'

'If the past doesn't get talked about then it gets forgotten. It'll be the same with Afghanistan and Iraq. They'll even forget Northern Ireland.'

'The Falklands ended ages ago. I'm sick of hearing about it. People don't want to listen to that stuff anymore.'

'That's the point—they *should* listen. It's what we had to do. And what we did mattered. We *won*.'

'It was worthless. All of it.'

'Not if you lived on those islands. And not if you had some idea of duty. The war was about being invaded by a foreign power. It was about people's rights and the kind of lives they want to lead. It was about their freedom.'

Debbie used to believe that too, but I can feel her tense up as if I've spoken the biggest lie of all.

'You think that freedom is what all wars are about,' she says flatly.

'Isn't it obvious?'

'Not to me. Not to other mothers. Alex didn't die for our freedom or anyone else's. There was nothing noble about the way he was sacrificed. I don't think he helped protect us here in the West. And let's face it, everything out there is backward and repressive and corrupt. We're not achieving anything by fighting and dying in that country.'

But I believe that we are. I believe that if we weren't there then people's lives would be so tormented they would be impossible.

'His death was pointless,' Debbie insists.

As though it is necessary to look Alex in the face as she speaks, she turns to study the photos on the table.

At the front of the display is a portrait of Alex in his uniform. He stands between us looking proud and happy. He knows he has made the right choice. His parents are proud, too, but although there is nothing hidden in my own face Debbie is unable to fully disguise her doubt. Even back then she was never persuaded that Alex had done the right thing.

'He was just in the wrong place at the wrong time,' she goes on, and her voice begins to shake. 'He shouldn't even have *been* out there. Whoever killed him did it from a distance. His murderer didn't look him in the eye. He didn't *choose* Alex. He won't have bad dreams about him. He didn't even know what Alex looked like.'

I say nothing.

'And when he was brought back, when he came back home, we weren't even allowed to see him.'

'It was maybe just as well.'

'I *know* that. But I wanted to. I *wanted* to.'

I do not answer. We both know that our son was scarcely recognisable.

Although we lived apart by then, Debbie and I had agreed that we should be together when Alex's personal possessions were returned. Every one of them felt like a blow.

Amongst them there was a surprise. Alex's girlfriend had walked out on him three months before he was killed, had not even attended his funeral, and yet we discovered that he still kept her photograph in his wallet. By then he must have meant nothing to her. Quite probably she had destroyed or hidden every image she had of him, and yet Alex still carried her portrait close to his heart. I looked at her face for a long time. Everything I touched was a message from the past.

In my war I had seen an enemy soldier hit by an incendiary flare. He screamed and ran without direction, his shocked friends backing away from this crackling torch, the blaze illuminating the ramshackle barricade until at last he collapsed on the ground. When we rushed forward his limbs were still thrashing and the sodden turf steamed around his body. The grey dawn smelled of peat and burned hair and phosphorus, but all sounds dropped beneath the heavy madness in my heart. Some of the men we bayoneted in the dugout. Others scrambled from it and fled. I followed one as he stumbled wildly across the bleak dark hill. His unfastened helmet toppled from his head and his coat flapped weakly around him like the wings of an injured bird. There was mist and smoke in my throat and the shrieks of the dying in my ears. I stopped and took aim. The man was in my sights. There was no escape. I knew I had him.

And suddenly he stopped and threw down his rifle, almost as if he had rehearsed the moment. It hit the turf with a curious flat motion. And then he turned and looked at me with wide, fearful eyes and an unshaven face whose skin was as white as bone. He jerked his hands upward like a parody of surrender. For a moment any sense of reality dropped away.

I did not lower my aim. The man said something but his words were as senseless as those spoken underwater. We stood there for moments that I could not measure.

And then he gradually lowered his right hand to indicate that he had an inside pocket. I did nothing. His eyes were pleading for mercy and I thought that maybe his lips were, too. I hated him for his eagerness to surrender and his desperate need to live.

Slowly he eased the hand into the pocket. I thought that he could be reaching for a photograph of his girlfriend but I also knew that a prisoner might suddenly withdraw a hidden pistol and shoot his captor dead. I knew I couldn't take that chance. I knew I couldn't hesitate.

I fired. The round hit him hard and he fell over backwards so rapidly and so ridiculously that his feet could have been hinged.

I never told Debbie the full truth of what had happened. I had once thought of telling Alex. Just before he left to go overseas I went for a drink with him and began to confess, but then I stopped. I would tell my son when he returned. But Alex never returned. A roadside bomb exploded beneath the wheels of his vehicle, tore it apart, and tossed its wreckage aside. Now I would never be able to confess to my son that I had once executed a captive. My Argentinean had been young, handsome, and unshaven, with frightened eyes. How could I have known that many years later he would return to invade my dreams?

'Whatever you say, the war was still worth it,' I tell Debbie. 'Maybe it's not your fault that you don't understand why. No one understands any more. People don't realise what's at stake.'

'You can think what you like. I can't stop you believing in things that aren't worth believing in.'

'And your new friend Vince agrees with you, does he? A man who's never had to fight a war—is that right?'

'*Most* of us have never had to fight a war, so that's a stupid thing to say, and you know that it is.' Debbie stands back to examine her work. 'You shouldn't try to annoy me. Never pick a fight with someone who could let you walk out with your hair part-done.'

A crazy part of me wonders if I should take the initiative and stand up and leave, no matter how the unfinished cut may look. But of course I don't. Instead we fall silent, and I pick anxiously at the slices of hair that have fallen on my sleeve.

After cutting for several more minutes Debbie announces satisfaction with her progress. 'That's better. Yes. All I need do now is tidy up the edges. And I'll sort out your ears, too. I've got a little machine for that. And I'll do your eyebrows while I'm at it.'

She puts the scissors back on the table and plugs in the clippers to a socket on the wall. The droning metallic buzz is close enough to sound threatening.

I use her name for the first time. 'Debbie.'

'What?'

'Have you invited Vince to move in?'

The clippers falter momentarily but then move on. Desperation silts my heart.

'He doesn't belong here,' I tell her.

'You can't hold back change.'

It's not the answer I want. It's not an answer at all. There's a taste in my mouth like a rotting tooth.

'Have you given him my key?'

'No. No, I haven't.'

The clippers crawl and buzz across my scalp as if I'm being prepared to join the ranks again.

'But you want him here, don't you?'

'I don't know. I really don't know. I'm not keen to invite anyone else to share my world. Especially after Alex.'

Vince never met Alex. I'm happy about that. I wouldn't want him to have known our son.

'It's the past that makes us what we are,' I say.

'You're wrong. It's the present. What we shared is past. Our marriage is past. Even Alex is in the past now. And we've got to learn to live in the present.'

And I think of Vince, a man I have never met, swaggering into property that I still think of as mine.

Debbie takes the clippers from my skin and steps back. My head tingles slightly and my limbs are weak. Strands of hair litter the sheet like plucked feathers from a bird.

'Eyebrows and ears,' she says.

She tilts my head as if it was inanimate and begins to slice away the tiny hairs on my ears. The cleaner's rotating blades deafen me. When she has finished Debbie lifts the scissors again and clicks them absentmindedly as she studies my eyebrows.

'I always used to cut Alex's hair, too, do you remember? When he was in his early teens he was desperate to be fashionable. I had to keep up with all the latest styles.'

'Of course I remember.'

'I looked after both of you, didn't I? Helped pick your clothes. Told you what suited you and what didn't. Made sure you always looked good. And Alex *always* looked the best.'

'That's right, he did.'

Light trembles on the scissor blades.

'Don't move,' Debbie says as I involuntarily flinch, 'I'm not going to harm you.'

'I know,' I say; 'I know.'

But I feel exposed and vulnerable and think that even someone in an everyday situation, like having a haircut, could be easily injured or killed. I am always having thoughts like this.

'There,' Debbie says after a another minute or so, 'you look fine now.'

Her voice is suddenly thin. She clears her throat roughly before she goes on.

'You look like a soldier again.'

I am not sure that it is meant to be a compliment. Debbie lifts the towel from my shoulders and gathers it together.

'I hope you're pleased,' she tries to add, but the words crack like ice beneath too heavy a weight.

I stand up and watch Debbie as she goes into the kitchen, bends to flip open the lid of a refuse bin, and shakes the gathering of cut hair into it. Afterwards she does not fully straighten, but remains slightly stooped and with her head bowed. I can hear the second hand of the kitchen clock as it ratchets across the numbers and divisions.

When Debbie speaks again her voice is thick, as if her throat is full.

'None of us can go back. We have to live with what we've got. The past is just the past. It's gone. We can do nothing about it.'

She raises her head and looks at me. Her face is set and her eyes have become suddenly angry.

'If I was offered a chance to go back then I'd take it,' she says. 'If someone came along and told me I could go back in time and change things then I would go. I wouldn't care about you or about me, I wouldn't care about anyone or anything else, I would only care about Alex. And I'd do everything I could to make sure that he was still alive. I'd sell my soul to do that, and I wouldn't care if it was to an angel or a demon.'

I don't know what how to answer. Maybe I shouldn't try. A few stray hairs have fallen on my trousers and I brush them away as if it mattered.

'You don't understand, do you,' she goes on. 'You got used to a soldier's life, you got used to people being killed. It's *natural* to you. Like part of the universe. But it'll never be natural to me. Alex needn't have been killed. His death was avoidable and unnecessary. He didn't save anyone or anything by dying.'

Debbie stops for a few seconds and it feels momentarily as if everything has been paused. And then she speaks again.

'Nothing will ever be worth the life of my son. You can tell me that it's for any cause you can think of, but I'll not believe it. I'll always say that you got fooled. The two of you. You got *fooled*.'

But I think that she knows nothing about either truth or death. Debbie's grief and her loss are all a bit unreal. She hasn't had to face death in the way that I've had to. I doubt if she's ever even seen anyone dead.

'You should go,' she says, as if everything between us has been exhausted.

I rub a hand across my scalp and feel the bristles. The cut has been close; just the way that I like it.

'I'll do that,' I say.

'I don't want you to come face to face with Vince.'

'Right.'

For a moment I stand there, for all the world as

though I was expecting to be invited back home, and as if somehow life could be restored to what it once had been.

'Please leave,' Debbie says; 'leave now.'

She walks behind me to the door. Outside it is still raining. I put my coat and hat back on in a silence that seems to bulk around us. I don't know what to say, and instead I nod curtly. Even as I do that, I know it's wrong.

The moment that I step back into the drizzle the door closes behind me. Without thinking I check in my pocket for the keys, but I gave them up months ago. The damp air feels cold in my lungs and my scalp tingles a little.

I start walking. I think that maybe on the other side of the door Debbie has begun to cry again. It comes easy to her, but it's difficult for me.

After less than a minute a decelerating car drives past, its indicator flashing. Behind the sweep of the wiper blades a man's face can be seen through the smeared windscreen. He is middle-aged and undistinguished and I wonder if it is Vince. But I do not turn to see where the car stops. Instead I try to increase my stride and walk on. We'll meet face to face sometime. It can't be avoided. We'll sort things out then. Sometimes it's necessary to delay facing things.

I didn't fully understand what I was doing on that island, but I knew we were there because it was necessary. Besides, I'd signed up to fight whenever and wherever I was told to fight. I left the reasons to others. Maybe the dead Argentinian had been just like me. We fought and we died for an idea of moral right that we never really thought about and only partly understood.

He lay on the blank dark hillside with his head tilted back and his dead eyes staring up into dark low cloud. There was several days' growth of beard on his chin and for the first time I noticed that his unkempt hair needed

61

cutting. As a colourless dawn edged across his body it seemed to gather its shape.

I bent down to study the hand that was slipped into his inside pocket. Only the wrist was fully visible. I pressed the clothing on his chest where a pistol could be hidden and it was wet with blood. There was no sign of any firearm.

I tugged at his arm and the hand slid free. A photograph was clenched between his thumb and first two fingers. The blank side was facing upwards, and on it was written a message in a language that I did not understand. I took the photograph from the dead man's fingers and turned it over. It was a portrait of a man and woman in their forties; his parents.

I put the photograph back in his tunic and pressed the sodden clothing back down on it. Light was strengthening and the man's face was taking on more detail and more personality. I turned away. I already knew too much about him.

He'd been terrified of death, I thought. My captive hadn't wanted to live and fight on that bleak cold island, miles away from home. He was there because he had to be. Maybe in those last few seconds he'd understood what things were really like. Maybe just before he died he could have seen in my eyes that I had cause enough to kill him. I was right. I'd always been right. Justice was on my side. And maybe in those last few seconds my captive saw that, too.

ADAM MAREK

# Dinner of the Dead Alumni

TODAY THE STREETS of Cambridge are crawling with dead alumni. Their ghosts perch on punts, trailing their fingers through the green weed without raising a ripple. They fly round Trinity College's Great Court, performing the 367m run before even the tenth of the twenty-four chimes. They cheer themselves, but their cheers reach no corporeal ears. The dead waft through the Grand Arcade, raising goosebumps on the fresh navels of girls texting outside Topshop. They hover at the doorway of the Apple store, whooping every time a fresh burst of radio waves casts them across the concourse and dashes their weightless bodies on the ground.

Preston cannot see them, but ever since he and Yolanda arrived with their twin girls, he has been aware of something funky in the air.

Static discharges from the ghosts of Trinity College have horripilated every hair on his body, and it is these upright antennae that have made him as sensitive as a flytrap. This hypersensitivity allows Preston to notice, for the first time, the unearthly magnetism of Kelly from all the way across the Apple store.

Something about Kelly wakes up his belly button. It blinks and blinks as if this is the first girl it has ever seen.

Preston knows her name is Kelly because that is what it says on her badge. Her job title though, two point sizes smaller, defies both his eyes and his belly button. To all seeing parts of his body, she is just Kelly, dark curls tumbling at her neck, wearing a helter-skelter of candy stripes. Preston falls all the way down her and leaves his breath at the top.

When she puts down the iPhone and leaves the shop, Preston cannot help but follow.

Yes, Preston is married. Yes, he has twin girls. Here they all are, coming out of the Grand Arcade public toilets, stopping to watch the teenage boy with the bright orange hair run at the wall, bound up its surface, and then flip himself over. The rubber soles of his Converse boots slap the pavement with a sound that knocks olives from ciabattas. Even the ghosts stop to watch the boy. Here is an amazed Bertrand Russell with his arms folded across his chest.

The twins, Libby and Daniela, are lively now they've peed. Their fingers are still wet from washing, pulling at the ties of Yolanda's top, snapping threads, until Yolanda smacks the back of their hands and begs them to leave her alone for just one moment.

The girls have dried ice cream around their mouths. There is something porcine in the flair of their nostrils. These are identical twins. If they were even a little different, they would not draw stares the way they do. Yolanda tries to ignore the people who are so fascinated by her uncanny younglings. She holds their hands high enough to prevent mischief and marches them through the arcade towards the Apple store.

❧

Today, the Master of Trinity College has invoked the memory of the dead. It is 350 years since the college's greatest alumnus, Isaac Newton, first attended the college, and it is 100 years since Ludwig Wittgenstein first came to the campus. A moment in time worthy of marking. Living alumni from around the world have come to Cambridge to celebrate, elbow to elbow with the dead.

In the chapel, delighted tourists startle Newton's statue with their camera flashes. One Vietnamese lady is so excited, she feels herself re-made by Trinity's architecture. Something of its grandeur has straightened her spine. She pokes her enormous glasses hard against her face. Now Cambridge is inside her, proud and worthy. Its lawns lay down for her. This is where she will send the children she has yet to conceive, *if* they don't get into Hogwarts.

All around Cambridge, in halls and houses, blue gowns are pulled over heads. Trinity's wizards group together where they find each other on the streets. A magical fraternity, for whom Wordsworth's 'Loquacious clock' speaks, so special even the sun has got its hat on.

In Trinity College Hall, high up in the rafters, a wooden mallard listens to the sounds of cutlery being placed far below, and to the percussion of crockery rolling like spun pennies at each of the guests' places.

Distracted like this, the duck does not notice AA Milne and Jawaharlal Nehru behind it whispering to each other and giggling, wondering if, between them, they can conjure enough solidity in their fingertips to break this bird's inertia.

We must feel sorry for this mallard, who has been moved from rafter to rafter by ingenious pranksters for decades. Who has watched bread broken by England's best minds from vertiginous heights, while not one crumb has ever been cast in its direction.

Kelly moves fast in heels, even over cobbles. Preston weaves around the tourists, keeping her candy stripes in sight. To understand why he chases her vapour trail like this, you must know about a girlfriend Preston had when he was sixteen. She told him something that would haunt him for ever.

Her name was Annabel, and she was a violent kisser who left his lips swollen and tender and tasting of cherry Chapstick. He cannot think about her without hearing the sound of incisors clashing. She told him that for every person, there is a partner so perfect that if you touch them, you'll both orgasm immediately.

Preston had many questions about Annabel's myth, such as, would orgasm occur *every* time these two people touched each other? If, say, the magic happened in a train carriage where the two people were standing, and the rocking of the train was knocking them together again and again, would they come repeatedly? Was the effect expendable? Annabel had only a surface knowledge of this phenomenon and was unable to answer his questions.

He and Annabel did not share this magical property. They worked each other sore to reach such climaxes. But this idea stayed with him, fascinated him, throughout his life. The assessment of girls for this property was simple and discreet and he conducted it frequently. Obsessively. He did it in pubs, in queues at the cinema, at the super-market, never finding her.

His relationships were always short. To him, they could only be temporary because despite their individual merits, what was the point in being with anyone but his absolute perfect match?

It sounded to Preston like a most inconvenient gift, and

yet he yearned for it. An orgasm that one did not have to work for, that came unsolicited at some unsuspecting moment, would surely be the most wondrous of all.

Throughout Preston's thirty-two years, he had sloughed the beliefs of his youth, leaving the most outrageous first. He skipped over Santa and crunched fairies and were-wolves beneath his boots when he was still wearing size 4s. He stomped on people who could move objects with their minds and did not look back.

But this one belief, in the spontaneous orgasm of two people perfectly attuned to each other, stayed with him. It had been so appealing to his 16-year-old mind, and it was so impossible to disprove by scientific study, that he clung to it. The last piece of magic on Earth. And today, the day that Trinity's dead walk the streets of Cambridge, he feels more certainly than ever before that he has found his orgasmic twin.

Already the blood has rushed from his head into the divining rod which he follows through the market square crowds, past stalls of ostrich meat and novelty Obama t-shirts and Jamaican patties, so enchanted that he ignores the rational part of his mind that reminds him about Yolanda.

Yolanda arrives at the Apple shop. She scans the top of people's heads, because Preston is taller than most men, but he is not there. She moves around the big tables, and pulls the twins' hands away from the laptops, and tells the sales assistants with their weird hair and their informality that she needs no help. Maybe Preston has stooped to look at goodies he cannot afford. She moves through the whole shop twice, and then scans heads again, but he is not there.

Outside the shop, while she takes out her phone and

dials Preston's number, Libby and Daniela point amazedly at the ghosts, who are leaning into the wind of radio-waves pouring from the shop. The ghosts stretch their arms wide, their eyes closed with delight.

Galumphing down Trinity Street comes the ghost of Aleister Crowley, class of 1898, horny as a dunnock. How desperately he needs something, anything, to make naked magic with. But everywhere he looks, every phantasmic face to which he raises a cheeky eyebrow turns away. Where are all the lady-ghosts? And where are all the adventurous men? These ghosts are shameful in their conventionality.

Aleister bites at the air, bites ineffectually at the necks of the living, until, finally, a pair of luminous eyes meets his — another dead alumnus who has awoken from his sleep engorged, causing Aleister's ectoplasm to bubble.

These ghosts have no need for propriety. The last time either of them loved another like this it was illegal, but watch them now set upon each other's mouths with ravenous joy. Fingers groping through layers of refracted light. They drop to the ground, and there, at five-thirty on a Saturday afternoon in June, being walked through by students and tourists and terriers, they satiate each other.

Preston is startled by the vibration of his phone in his pocket, and then a second later, the ring begins — the opening beats of Michael Jackson's 'Billy Jean'. He takes the phone out, and on the screen is a photo of Yolanda he took last Christmas. She is poking her tongue out.

He lets the phone ring until his voicemail answers, and then he puts it back in his pocket. He will call her in a few minutes once he has decided how to explain that he has to catch up with this girl, lay his hand upon her, to test whether his instincts are correct, that this is the one person on the planet for whom he is specifically made. Surely a demonstration of two people enjoying simultaneous orgasm from one touch alone would negate the need for explanations and excuses? No one bound by mere marital and coincidental attachment could argue with something as miraculous as that.

But now . . . where is she? From the mouth of Rose Crescent, a tour group in matching purple jumpers has poured into Trinity Street, closing the gaps between bodies through which he was navigating, and despite his height, he has lost her.

Preston tries to push through the people like he is a ghost, like he will not bounce off them, but bounce off them he does, and soon, alerted by the angry grunts of people knocked aside, the crowd moves to let him through. To Preston, this almost biblical division of shoppers is another clear sign. The path is so clear that he is able to run, staring into every shop window for a second to see if she has gone inside. Every moment that he does not find her makes it more likely that he will never see her again.

Behind the college, on the river, a raft of punts nods into the weed as each of the students steps upon it. They take hands and help each other onto this buoyant stage, excited because this is the first time they have ever done it. On the banks, students and fellows and parents sit on tartan blankets popping corks and gouging stalks from the hearts of strawberries.

And here too there are ghosts, the angle of the sun turning their blue to gold. They watch the students and ache to feel once more the giddy thrill of an unsteady platform beneath their feet, the simple joy of something that confounds the senses.

Guys in gowns thrust poles deep into the Cam and guide the raft out to the middle. The singers arrange themselves by voice and height as they have rehearsed, and grin because these sensations are still novel.

When they are in position, they wait for a certain still-ness that is imperceptible from the bank, and then they open their mouths.

The pink bellows that cradle their lungs push out something so sweet it causes champagne pourers to over-fill their glasses, and even the dead to weep.

This sound is trampled in the marketplace, where Yolanda kneels before her girls. They have been fighting over Libby's Sea Monkeys keyring—a mini-aquarium the size of a child's fist filled with overfed brine shrimp.

Yolanda holds Daniela's forearm out to show Libby the deep red crescents which fit Libby's fingernails like a glass slipper.

It terrifies Yolanda that they fight like this. When the girls first became aware of each other, before they could even sit up, they would use their chubby little arms like clubs against each other, they would kick with their sticky feet, and they bit before they even had teeth. On their third birthday, Yolanda found Daniela crouched over Libby pressing a cushion onto her face.

Yolanda had suggested to Preston that they take the girls somewhere, to see someone, but he had been adamant that this is how kids behave. Every time the twins fight, Yolanda thinks about the barn owl chicks she saw on *Springwatch*, all hatched a week apart, of different sizes, like Matryoshka dolls, and how they did fit inside one another, because the largest chick ate the others alive. It tipped its head all the way back, shuddering with the effort of swallowing something only one size smaller than itself.

Yolanda calls Preston again, and again gets no answer. Behind her lips, her vitriol is rehearsing.

Mummy, Libby says, where are all those blue people going?

What blue people? Yolanda says.

And then Libby bolts, her greasy little fingers slipping easily out of Yolanda's hand.

Yolanda yells her name and runs after her as fast as Daniela's feet can keep up, but Libby whips round the knees of people in the market. Yolanda unpacks the voice she only uses at home when the curtains are closed, a full-force roar that reconfigures her face and terrifies the shoppers around her. When this sound hits one old dear, she falls into a display of honeydew melons, and they tumble together, bashed knees, bruised melons and a broken wrist. Yolanda picks up Daniela and runs after Libby whose white dress appears only every few seconds as gaps open up between people. Squeezed tight against Yolanda's chest as she runs, Daniela's feet jiggle above the street, whizzing past paper bags and wristwatches. Her chin is knocked by her mother's shoulder and her teeth slam together on her lip. As blood wells up through the split, she starts to howl.

Preston's ankle is throbbing. Weakened by a tennis injury, it cannot cope with these cobbles, but he pushes on. He would run on bloodied stumps if he had to.

Every one of his senses is tuned to the wavelength of red and white candy stripes and he scans the windows of Strada and Heffers and the Royal Bank of Scotland as he charges past. His body flushes with pleasure chemicals as he sees the briefest flash of candy-stripe fabric going through the Great Gate of Trinity College.

On the river, the choir has reached crescendo, their voices threaded together and cast over the bank-side audience, captivating them so deeply that even their breath needs permission.

The sound draws the dead from all over Cambridge. It awakens late risers from their beds—beds which have collapsed around their sleepers, so long have they slept.

The porters wearing their practised faces do not stop porting, but lift up the edges of their bowler hats to trap inside some of the music for later, when they can enjoy it in bare feet, patrolling their rooms with their belts unbuckled.

In the kitchens, the singing is barely audible amongst the sound of wooden spoons in pans, knives on chopping boards, bubbles struggling against glass lids. But it causes the crystal glasses to ring most eerily. It drives the ghost of Byron's bear crazy. Watch it gambol through the dining room, shaking its blue-bloodied muzzle, loping through the completed silver service. Not even the flames atop the candelabra notice it pass.

On the river, the last note pulls behind it a silence so deep and terrifying that every hand feels compelled to fill this void with the most reassuring applause it can muster.

At the Great Gate, Preston queues among the gowned fellows, his extraordinary height allowing him to see over the top of their heads into the Great Court, but his candy-striped girl has vanished.

He lets his phone ring until it tires in his pocket. He still does not have an explanation for Yolanda.

When he looks at his watch, he causes everyone around

him to look at their watches, and this need to know the time flows out from him in a great concentric wave, compelling everyone at that very moment to know the time. As if in answer, the clock above the Great Court chimes the hour twice over. It is six o'clock.

At the mouth of the Great Gate, beneath Henry VIII brandishing his wooden chair-leg, Preston notices for the first time that he is the only one in the queue not wearing a gown and the only one not carrying an invitation card.

On King's Parade, everyone stops to look at their watches together, and in this moment of stillness, they stare at Yolanda running. She is an impressive sight, her plaited ponytail slapping at her back. The cords in her neck come out to amplify her voice as she yells Libby's name. Her flip-flops slap the paving, ticking out the double chimes of Trinity's clock. And over her shoulder, Daniela, hypnotised by shaking, clings to her mother's chest, watching the amazed faces recede behind her.

Ahead of them, Libby chases the ghosts.

Now they have all arrived at the college, the living and the dead. The ghosts need no invitation, and melt through the queue like it's not there, melt through Preston, who is shuffling forward in the procession. He watches each person in front showing their invite to the porter. This porter looks like he is immune to bargaining. He has a big-chested solidity and eyes that have no whites. His mouth does not reciprocate smiles.

Preston apologizes as he cuts sideways through the crowd, towards a group of four younger men in gowns. One of them has some kind of colourful juggling equipment, and the others are gathered around him, examining it. Their conversation stops as he approaches, and their mouths open slightly when they appreciate his size. Preston hunches in the way that he does.

I've forgotten my invite, he says. And my gown. I'll give you two hundred quid for a loan of one of yours.

I don't get undressed for less than five hundred, the juggler-boy says laughing outrageously at himself. And I don't think it would fit you anyway. The laughter of the other boys spills all over the pavement, splashes against Preston who stands as still as a lighthouse, his face ignited. He retreats back into the queue, a full head taller than anyone else.

On the ground, Aleister Crowley's mouth is at the neck of his man, whispering incantations over his neon moles. This couple is insensible of footsteps and the heavy pendulums of carrier bags. Aleister's spell unwraps itself, a mischievous gift, something from the other side, loosening the screws of gravity.

Preston's fantastic height has caught the attention of the porter at the gate. Preston has seen him note the pink collar of his shirt—so alien among the starched-white-on-navy of the fellows' uniforms. Far ahead, through the arches of the fountain, climbing the stone steps to the Hall, is the candy-striped woman. She is now wearing a gown, and the fabric swishes about her, revealing slivers of her wonderful stripes.

Now the queue has narrowed at the mouth of the entrance. There are only three people ahead of Preston. Fear floods his system with something radioactive, something that burns at his joints. Fear of being turned away, and fear of never knowing whether this woman was the one.

The fear turns to energy and energy turns to action. To

the amusement of the fellows around him, Preston steps straight over the barrier and runs.

The porter calls out stop. Gives chase. Other porters come. Other men in gowns pursue him. But Preston is a daddy long-legs, each of his strides covering three of a normal man's. He pounds across the lawn, past the fountain. Those behind him cannot keep up, and those ahead of him stand aside for fear of the violent strength such a giant could command.

For the second time today, a path clears for Preston.

He leaps up the stone steps in a single bound, into the corridor, past the ghosts of Newton and John Dryden and Francis Bacon who stand before their portraits imitating their own expressions.

He ducks low through the entrance to the Hall, and two hundred faces all turn towards him.

Trinity Street is awash with gowns and chatter, and in this confusion, Yolanda has lost sight of Libby. She imagines someone, some dribbling, broken-toothed paedophile putting pawprints on her white dress and over her mouth. Faced with this terrifying vision she stops and gathers up everything she has inside her. Her yell is so fierce it moves through the crowd like a shockwave. Ankles, unbolted by Aleister Crowley's tongue, betray their owners. Yolanda's ululation fells everyone. Every knee, every hip, every elbow and every shoulder on Trinity Street, in one great wave hits the pavement. There is a collective groan as the force of the fall pushes air from the lungs of more than three hundred people.

At the end of her scream, Yolanda's teeth sing like a tuning fork.

Before the fallen pick themselves up, while they are too shocked to even apologise to those they have scratched and groped as they fell, the only person standing is Libby, and an orchard of ghosts who stand rooted to the stones, staring at Yolanda. The force of her howl against their backs was a delicious sensation worth all of those numb decades.

Amongst them, Libby is staring at her smashed keyring aquarium, crying.

In the rafters, the mallard watches the colossus step into the room, and is suddenly airborne. Its wings are moulded firmly to its sides and all attempts to flap are futile. It watches the room turn around it, sees far above, its former perch and behind it, AA Milne and Jawaharlal Nehru high-fiving each other in delight. And then it crashes to the ground.

This isn't how Preston wanted this moment to be.

Standing in the middle of Trinity's fellows, ten feet tall and clutching a Waterstone's bag, sweaty from the pursuit, he scans the room and finds his girl. The timing of the duck's fall is so precise that there is a common misperception that he has knocked his head against the rafters and dislodged it.

The porters have waited moments while they gathered together in enough numbers to tackle this monster. Eight of them move in on him. Preston sees the girl, sitting on a bench close-by. One leg is crossed over the other, revealing a bare knee so smooth that his gaze can't settle upon it without sliding down her shin.

His insides are a-shiver. Closing the gap between himself and Kelly in two great strides, he takes in all of her. He can imagine the weight of her curls against his face, the plush smothering smack of her lips.

She recoils as he approaches, sliding her bottom along

the bench, but already he is there. For the first time he is able to read the rest of her name badge: Dr Kelly Campbell, Dept of Physics.

It will all make sense in a moment, he tries to say, but he is panting and his words come out all mashed into one. He could never have imagined that this moment of revelation, which should be spectacular for them both, would have happened with an audience. But somehow it is fitting.

Preston reaches out and wraps his long fingers around Kelly's wrist. She tries to pull away, and even stands up, but it is too late. The magic is already happening.

The sensation begins simultaneously in Preston's balls and his feet, rocketing through his insides, hormonal fireworks fizzing against the underside of muscles and curling round bones, making his titanic cartilage groan with pleasure.

He is compelled to close his eyes, to fully savour the fanfare that is boiling in his underpants, but he does not. Something is wrong.

Kelly is still trying to wrestle free from his grip. Her face shows no sign of supernatural ecstasy. Only horror.

Preston is coming alone.

It is too late to stop. Even if he let go of her now. His insides are on fire and the fire will not stop until he is all ashes. He has never felt an orgasm like this before. Hidden fuses throughout his systems flare and blow. Cells chime against cells. The pleasure is uncontainable, and his terror makes it even sweeter. Terror because now he sees all around him the blue faces of Trinity's past. Lights obscure his vision. His knees crumple. He is unmade.

Even knelt like this before Kelly, he is still taller than her. And her expression is one of revulsion.

Porters have his collar, have his arms, grab his fingers

and force them to relinquish Kelly. Yank him backwards with such velocity he is forced to run on his heels. Men and women gather round Kelly, healing her with their murmurs, and block her from Preston's view.

As the orgasm, the most tremendous orgasm in the universe, subsides, a sense of abjection washes in to fill the space it has left.

The porters drag Preston down the stone steps, across the lawn, to the front gate where queuing fellows still wait. For the third time today, the crowd divides to allow him through.

When Yolanda reaches Libby, the shoppers have stood up and are brushing themselves down, looking around to see what has happened. Maybe they suspect a bomb has gone off. But as soon as the first person has resumed shopping, the others follow, and within seconds, it's as if Yolanda's utterance never existed.

Libby is on her knees, sobbing, picking up the fractured pieces of her Sea Monkeys keyring from the ground. In between cobbles, the little brine shrimp twitch their tails, their segmented legs working the meniscus of their spilled environment.

Yolanda sets Daniela down on the ground. And now that the adrenaline is retreating back into the caves of her body, she feels all the muscles she has pulled in her pursuit. Something holding her spine straight has snapped. Something in her thigh is burning. She is conceiving Libby's punishment when among the crowd of strangers she sees Preston. His walk is weird and hobbled.

I'm sorry, he says.

Yolanda starts in with the where have you beens and I've been going crazy I've just had to chase our daughter through the street do you have any idea what . . . and then she stops because Preston is wearing a familiar expression which she can't quite place.

I don't feel so good, he says.

Why are you walking funny? What the hell happened to you?

Preston needs time to concoct an explanation. I'm okay, he says. Let's just go home.

But this is not acceptable to Yolanda, and she shifts tack on the questions and suggests scenarios to Preston to which he must reply yes or no. Have you been attacked? Have you had an aneurysm? This method of elimination is unlikely to reveal the exact circumstances which have led Preston to be standing here, concealing a sticky patch of semen from the world with a carrier bag, but Yolanda is relentless.

In the Hall, Preston's fingerprints have faded from Kelly's arm. The mallard has been set upon the head table beside a basket of rolls. The gravy is thickening in the pot. The singers are back on the bank. Byron's bear is cavorting unseen in the river. Aleister and his mate lay on their backs looking up through the people at the blushing sky. They are breathless. The master of Trinity tings his glass three times with a teaspoon. This dinner of the dead alumni has begun most memorably.

SJ BUTLER

# The Swimmer

THE ALDERS AT the river's edge stand motionless in the midsummer heat. In the fields, the twisted cattle beans are black. A car buzzes out of sight, its engine muzzled by the thick air. Above it all, the sky is a bleached starling's egg blue. Three weeks of windless sun weigh down on the fields; nothing moves except the water, slow, steady, a slick of olive green pouring away from her.

She sits at her desk in the back room gazing out at the river. Where it rounds the first bend there's an eddy as the current twists out into the middle, pirouettes and continues on its course. The sun catches the ripples, sprays them silver for a moment. The light is so bright that she can hardly bear to look at it.

She is so hot.

No one has passed for at least three hours. Even the fishermen have stayed at home. The fish, and the fishermen, prefer the rain, she thinks — on wet days she sees the men trudging out from the road, lugging bags, boxes and umbrellas out of sight along the river path. Not today. It's too hot. The fish will be lying safe in the cool soft mud on the river's bottom.

No one's out there. If she goes now, she'll have the

river to herself. No one will see. Why she minds this, she doesn't know. Every day she looks out at the river, and longs to swim in it.

Why hasn't she swum before? People have swum in rivers for generations. It's a normal, natural act.

And today she is so hot. The river is there, waiting. Today it is slow and peaceful and no one will see her.

She gathers her towel and costume and, from the back of the cupboard, her old plimsolls. She changes, puts her shorts and T-shirt back on top, ties her hair back. She checks her messages, shuts her office door, heads downstairs and drinks a glass of water. She steps out into the heat, feels sweat prickle all over her body. Heavy, sultry air clamps her head, her limbs. Her thoughts are squeezed in a fist.

Out on the river path she takes long fast steps. Her shoes kick up pale dust which coats her legs and sticks to the sweat. Her nostrils itch, suck in pollen, dust, humid air, the dirty yellow smell of ripening stems and grains. Grasshoppers scratch and whirr, invisible in the tangled grass; one leaps onto the path in front of her, and on again to a new blade of grass. A sturdy spider runs out of a crack in the earth, and runs back in six inches further along. She barely registers them. Her thoughts pull to and fro like overworked dough, a sticky grey mess of deadlines and undefined anxiety.

She rounds the first bend in the river. A curtain of grasses, reeds and willowherb hides the eddy she watches from her window. Through it, tiny glimpses of light and green water glitter.

Ahead, the second bend tugs the path in an extravagant right-hand swoop, swinging it into the field. An unnamed fear stirs her thoughts, takes a shape. Is the current stronger than it looks? In spate she has seen great branches, dead sheep even, swept past her window in seconds. Might it be too strong for her even today? Where might she be swept to?

She came this far once before, with her costume and towel. She stood and looked at the water, watched it flow, and her fears overwhelmed her. She turned back.

She doesn't look at the water today. She doesn't give it time. She reaches out for the alder tree, swings down to the mud beach on the curve of the river. Dried webbed footprints scurry over it. Already it's cooler down here by the running water.

She pulls off her clothes and shoes. Crouches down and reaches out her hand to feel the water. It is gloriously fresh as she pulls her fingers through it. The water is opaque, swirling with tiny particles, a dirty muddy green from the soil it carries. She stands, stretches one foot out into the water. It finds fine velvet silt which creeps between her toes and caresses her instep. A weed tangles a finger round her ankle then releases it as the current gently eases past her. She steps deeper, the water lapping her knees now, her shins glimmering like great vertical fish coming up for air from the green depths. Another step and all of a sudden there is no bottom, the beach is gone, and she sinks, arms reaching out and finding just water and then remembering to pull and stroke and swim.

Gasping, her hot skin shocked by the cold river, but exhilarated and woken from the sweltering daze that had taken her over, she takes stock. The water is deep, but she can easily tread water. She tries swimming upstream against the current, measuring her progress against the roots of the alder she climbed down—even here on the bend, where she can see the current moving across the river, she can make her way back to the beach without effort.

Encouraged, she decides to swim upstream as far as the bridge behind her house. Then she'll turn back and return to her desk in time to start the afternoon's work. She kicks out, and turns upriver.

Down here at water level, she realises, not only is she invisible to the rest of the world, but it is invisible to her. The tops of the banks are at least ten feet above her so all she can see is the river, the banks and the sky. Her focus narrowed, she begins to notice tiny details: here where the river is kinked around a root, there are weeds with narrow dark green leaves. In places the banksides have been scraped back to bare earth by the spring floods, and high up there are clusters of miniature animal holes. At the water's edge there are more footprints, some webbed — both large and small — and some like the garden bird prints she sees at home. There are fishing weights tangled in tree roots. Thistledown floats in drifts across the water's surface.

Swimming is easier than she expected and soon she sees her bridge. Stalactites hang where the lime mortar has dripped over the decades. In the bridge's shadow she shivers — this is a place that the sun never warms and even today it is chilled, somewhere things come to hide. So she swims on, out the other side and back into the sunshine, glad now to feel its heat on her face and its dazzling reflection off the water. On she goes, up past the end of her garden — she can just make out the pile of lawn clippings she tipped over the fence. Her neighbours have built steps down the bank, she sees. Do they swim too?

The river widens ahead, and her toes catch the bottom if she lets her legs drift down. The water here is almost warm, spreading itself out in the sun. She slows her stroke, relaxing as the current releases its pressure, lazily making her way up to the next bend. The balsam is luxuriant here, a huge forest casting its sickly scent over the river.

She follows the curve, watching the water ripple around her arms as they stretch out in front of her, rising to the surface on the out stroke, sinking below into obscurity as she pulls back. She's quite unready for the swan. It's floating midstream, in profile, unmoving although under the surface it must surely be paddling. It doesn't see her at first—but her gasp of pleasure at its beauty alerts it to the strange sight of a swimmer in its river. It turns, majestic, slow, miraculously white in these silty surroundings. She had never before realised the sheer size of a swan. Down here, on its level, she is insignificant. There is no doubt in her mind whose territory this is.

She stops swimming, treads water, and gazes at the swan. Its body is almost as big as her own and its neck stretches three, maybe four feet above her, taut, elegantly curved, still. The swan looks down at her and she looks away, afraid to meet its eye. Her nan used to tell her a swan could break a man's arm with its wing—what could it do to her, down here, in the water?

Not daring to turn her back on the swan, she makes the tiniest movements, pulling herself away downstream, careful not to splash, barely blinking. The swan continues to watch her, minutely twisting its neck as she moves slowly across its vision. She wishes it would turn and look upstream. There's nowhere for her to hide. She drops down so that the water covers her mouth and cloaks her shoulders in green silk. The current pulls her towards the bank, and then with a sudden swirl back into the deep water and around the bend. Only now that the swan is out of sight does she turn away.

She drifts slowly under the bridge, letting the current pull her downstream. She feels the swan sweep down the river with her, its eyes on the back of her neck, pursuing her. When she twists round, though, it is nowhere to be seen.

She hardly needs to paddle. The languid summer current pulls her easily, and she once again passes the weeds, animal holes and tracks of her outward journey. Back at her beach she climbs out onto the dried mud and stands dripping for a moment before clambering back up the bank. The sun dries her skin instantly, so she pulls her clothes on over her costume and heads back home.

She cannot stop thinking about the swan. She sees the angle of its neck, the curve of its wing, its eye watching her, even as she works in her sweltering tiny office. It is still unbearably hot. And now the image of the swan makes it even harder to concentrate, so she promises herself another swim, at nightfall.

As the long midsummer day stretches on, she knows she cannot wait until the light fades, so while the evening still shimmers with heat she returns along the bank and drops back into the water, shuddering again at the cold. She swims up to the bridge, relishing the slow warmth of the shallows beyond it, letting the current stroke her skin, but then turns back downstream. Though she wants to see the swan, she doesn't want to offend it nor to tempt it to anger.

For the next five days the heat builds. She swims before breakfast, when the fields are still veiled with river mist and the air has a brush of cool left from the night. Downstream she finds a stretch of water that catches the morning sun, and as she swims on her back she can watch the broken water behind her glittering gold in the mist. At lunch she simply dips into the pool by her beach, washing the sweat from her skin, feeling the cool water reach into her core as she dives, eyes open, into a dusky world of half-seen shapes and gurgles: weeds reaching out their fingers, fish slipping past in a second, twigs and leaves tumbling to the bottom as she stretches her body, feeling her strength growing with each stroke, merges into the river.

The evenings are reserved for the swan. She finds that if she never fully enters its stretch of water, it simply turns its head slightly to watch her. It never moves towards her. It doesn't hiss, nor arch its wings. It remains untouched by her presence.

On the first evening it is just above the bridge, as before. They watch each other for a while, then the swan slides away upstream.

The next evening, she swims into the swan's curve of river, slowing so as not to threaten it, breathing quietly, careful not to splash. The swan isn't there. So she swims on, at each new bend anticipating the gleam of white feathers in the beginnings of dusk. And there it is, in the distance, at the end of a long straight, turning on the spot as though playing with an eddy. It doesn't see her at first and she watches as the light drops and the birds and insects fall gradually silent — the small patch of whiteness is all she can see by the time she lets the current turn and carry her home.

The days become fluid and she spends more time in the river. She is no longer afraid of anyone coming. Fishermen go upriver in the early morning but she doesn't care. Her skin and hair exude a smell of soil, weed and raw water. She barely works. She floats for hours, eyes closed against the dazzling sky, listening to the reeds slithering against each other and the water cluttering through tiny channels amongst roots and weeds. Or turns to face down, the current flowing past her as she hovers, suspended above the fish. She returns home to eat and to wait until evening when she can swim upstream to gaze at the swan before drifting back down, carrying its image home with her.

The sky is beginning to tinge a darker blue when she steps again into her pool, sinking into the water to escape the evening midges. She swims steadily upstream, familiar with each bend, bank and tree. Under the bridge the swifts screech and swoop after flies. She swims on, across the shallow water and around the bend.

She swims round the next bend, and the next, till she reaches the long straight where the swan twisted in its eddy. And there it is. It is twisting again, its white feathers stark against the dark of the water and the reeds. She swims nearer. The swan's neck is stretched taut. Its body writhes beneath it. She sees a webbed foot. She dares not move closer. As she watches in the fading light the swan grows calmer, though its neck reaches out still in a sharp diagonal. She waits. Whilst the swan has seemed to accept her, she knows she is deceiving herself if she thinks it her friend.

As dark falls the swan becomes still and she swims slowly towards it, barely rippling the water. It must see her coming. She swims another stroke closer. It seems to try to turn. The first moonlight touches its wings.

She pauses. Watches. She swims close enough to reach out and touch the swan. And finally she sees that it is trapped, bound in a web of glistening nylon fishing lines. They have slung it up by the neck and caught its great wings half outstretched. Its only movement is caused by the eddy curling beneath it.

She reaches up and strokes its neck, running her water-logged fingers over its smooth hardness. It is warm. Gently she starts to unravel the line, swimming round and round the great bird to set it free, pulling the thread from its wings, untangling the dangling feet, wrapping it in loops around her neck as she goes. Finally the swan's wings settle onto its back, crooked and disjointed. Now it is held only by its neck, where it must first have been caught as it flew down onto the water. Once again she swims round and round the swan, untwisting the line where the bird bound itself in its struggle. Finally, at the base of its neck, her fingers creep into finer feathers, seeking out the buried nylon. It is embedded in the soft flesh and she pulls it free. Warm blood mingles with the river water and washes over her.

She moves aside and lets the current take the bird. It drifts slowly down the straight, picked out against the dark water by the moonlight. As it rounds the bend she lets the current take her too, washing her downriver in the wake of the swan. She catches a glimpse of white as she drifts under the bridge but it is faint now, a puff in the distance. And at the next bend she cannot tell it from the mist rising from the water.

## HEATHER LEACH

# So Much Time in a Life

To begin with there were three children. The first, a girl with hair so dark and wet that, as she came out of me, it looked like a seal pelt: the sleek fur of a creature slipping from its underwater world onto the soft rock of my breast. The second was also a girl. Pale and fair-haired, she looked like me, familiar and human from the start. Perhaps this birth was easier, as people say the second often is, the love less fierce and fearful, but warm as sunlight, as basic as bread.

The third, a boy. What to say about him? His name: John? Adam? Sam? Something plain and unpretentious, my husband said. Nothing the other kids can hurt him with. Boys with weird names have it hard in the world. I could never get a name to stick: *the youngest, the littlest, the last*—these were the only names I gave him. He was the baby, that's all. When you have two already, a new child needs time to grow into its particular space in your mind, to make itself real. Alive.

Imagine the mother as about thirty-five, bouncy haired and nicely ordinary. Not too clever, but definitely not stupid. She has to work of course, but always makes sure she gets off early to pick the kids up, her two girls, four

89

and seven from school. She runs some kind of office . . .
a solicitor's? An architect's? No, she has to have something more about her than that. Depth and definition.
She could work for Greenpeace or Friends of the Earth,
got the job by chance because the other candidates were
too surly and she made the interviewers laugh. She never
started out political; in fact she used to think politics was
the biggest turn-off since Y-fronts but now she . . .

Look, is this the cat's mother? Give the woman a
proper name. Alice, Emma, Jane? Jaqueranda? Get a grip,
much too over the top. On the other hand, she could be
Jack for short. Fashionably cross-gender without being in
your face butch. Let's say she had an odd mother which
explains the name. This mother, conveniently dead now,
was a touch eccentric, a wannabee telly luvvie, six months
on *EastEnders*, not much else. *My promise was never fulfilled,
darling, etcetera etcetera.* Far too much emotion around the
breakfast table, far too many embarrassing clothes and gestures but this abfab background accounts for the steely but
hidden potential that Jack—short for Jaqueranda—will
have to draw on later when what happens happens.

Fiction is an evasion, a way of stepping out of your
own life and into another's, of making things work out,
connect, make sense. You see it in the paper. The house
burns down; a van rolls into a lake; a man takes them out
for the day, parks the car in a country lane and then he . . .

You think: those lovely children. How could she go
on after that?

My eldest girl became a beautiful child. Dark sea-green
eyes with spiky lashes. I did all the things that mothers do.
I held her in my arms. I fed her. I washed and dressed her.
She learned to look into my face, to put her small hand

onto my cheek. There was a connection, I'm sure there was. A touch.

November's a hard month, the hardest, Jack thinks, and of course it's raining as it seems to have done every day for almost a year. She's waiting outside the school gate in an unflamboyant jacket, jeans and shoes. She stands, calm and stylishly simple in the steamy petrol–fume fug a little distance away from all the other mothers, half-listening to them talk about the new teacher, the weather, this and that.

*. . . she seems OK, a bit snotty do you think, still you need them strict, I couldn't keep that lot in order, could you, it's enough trouble with one, thank christ I'm not a teacher, who would? . . . and the rain, my god, the bloody rain, will it ever stop, floods again all over, China, Germany, we'll have webbed feet next, you can't get dry, it's global, they're always saying something, you don't know whether to . . . bother much with cooking these days, too busy with, thank god for Burgernet . . . I said to her, look Michael's had a really bad throat and I'm not sure if he'll . . .*

Rain isn't bad if you're well wrapped, she thinks. She watches the water run down the railings the way she used to as a child: close up with full attention. She notes the orderly patience of each particular raindrop as it follows the others down into a tiny pool at the fence's foot.

There are no men today. You do get the odd chap, even two on occasions, a few on Fridays. More do the morning deliveries but the feminisation of the workplace hasn't stretched yet to letting the men off at half-past three, an irritating irony not lost on Jack as she stands beneath the battered and ragged horse chestnut, the light dissolving around her, the talk turning to Christmas and the lateness of things.

She does have a man of her own, a partner, the father of the children. But let him be vague and shadowy, let this be his only part, that he is the ground and boundary of her ordinariness which is meant to guarantee safety on this ordinary day.

The children are late coming out. The deputy head is delayed in ringing the bell, then they have to fasten their coats properly because of the rain. So, there are a few extra moments of waiting, for which she's grateful. She looks up through the tree into the latticed sky, observing line and interconnection: sky, wood, branch, the greyness of the tree trunk, the brown papery leaves like dead skins clinging. All around her the women ratchet up the Christmas mill:

*. . . how they'll have to start soon, the terribleness of it all beginning again, who's done what, who doesn't even want to think about it, and there's so much to do, so much to buy, god oh god oh god . . .*

The second girl is like a version of myself. The same way of turning her head, the exact same shape of the fingers, earlobes, skull. With this one, I have to be careful not to gather her back into me as if we were one life again. I was a good mother to her, I think. I let her grow into herself. Perhaps she even hates me for a while, that sameness a challenge. Ah, but those sweet first years. Even now I feel the weight of her small body asleep on my lap, while the other, my seal-girl leans against me, my arm safely around her.

The door of the school opens and the children run out, although Jack can't see hers yet. There's the usual huddle and muddle, some with coats half on, scarves dragging in puddles, hugs and kisses, questions and nags. Women are turning, *bye, see you tomorrow, bye,* already walking away, the children scrabbling to catch up, to hold on, the little gathering splitting into smaller and smaller groups, push-chairs across the road, cars revving, *hold tight I told you*, and as the moment on the pavement is over, a quietness begins to fall.

Jack waits, not looking at the school, or at the play-ground, let them come in their own time, no need to rush. She hears their footsteps before she sees them, the two girls hand in hand, the older looking after the younger, but still she doesn't let herself look, holding the moment as long as she can. Water runs down the railing, frayed leaves crackle in the tree.

*Look, Mum, somebody's lost that.*

A glove on the ground.

*Can we have some sweets?*

*Maybe, put your hood up, Alice, your hair's getting wet.*

*Slithery slidey,* says Kate, shuffling her feet through the leaves, *we've been making Christmas cards, can I have a Nin-tendo?*

These are the last children to come out, the final two, there is absolutely nobody else left and the three of them, Jack Jaqueranda, Alice and Kate walk slowly away along the pavement leaving me at the gate.

Leaving me here at the gate again where I shouldn't be, where I promised absolutely that I wouldn't go, agreed it was bad for me, that some of the other women thought it was odd, almost scary, and here she comes, the head teacher, clip-clopping across the school yard towards me with that sickeningly compassionate smile.

When is the moment when she becomes I? Is this it? They say that most people hate it, the author stepping into her story, spoiling the fictional dream. I hate it too, but here she is, here I am, breaking, breaking, breaking the frame. Something is going to happen to Jack. To her children. To the girls, dark and light, like sisters in a fairy story. To the unnamed boy, waiting to be picked up from the Children's Centre nursery.

She walks away from the school along the pavement, bending to listen to their stories of the day, all the time keeping a tight hold on those small woolly-gloved hands. Every day of that autumn term the same routine. Sometimes it rained. Sometimes it didn't. When she arrives at the nursery, her boy is riding a tiny push-along bike that he's wanted to play with all day and only now, when the bigger children have gone, can he get his chance. So he screams when Jack picks him up, fights and kicks as she fastens him into the push-chair, won't smile at the girls, nor give them a kiss, won't wave to the nursery nurse at the door, and howls and howls all the way back to their house.

I try not to follow. I try hard to stay here, behind this page and hidden in language, to keep out of her sight and her mind, as she stands on the step and starts the complicated business of trying to locate her door key in the multiple and stuffed-full sections of her bag, her many pockets, the bottom tray of the push chair, the bag on the back of the push-chair, oh god, why does she never remember where it is? It's the same every day, and now there's a scene, as the girls, tired and hungry, start shoving each other and the rain comes down harder and harder, swept in on a cold Atlantic wind, driven in from the west.

Inside the house, Jack struggles them out of their wet clothes and all three run about the house while she sets out drinks and snacks. She should do something creative with them, she thinks. Drawing or something. A game at least.

But it was a hard day at work and she has a meal to cook and sod it, she's tired, they'll have been doing that kind of stuff all day. Switch on the telly. CBeebies. They sit and watch, all three in a row, quiet now and dozy, munching on raisins and crisps. She stands in the window looking out on the street.

Then there were two. Women start later, these days. The career ladders. The glass ceilings. Only so much time in a life. It was hard to choose. Everybody, even if they don't admit it, would like one of each. A girl and a boy. What could be better? So the dark girl had to go. She was beautiful, true, but she always seemed strange, never quite mine. I gave her back to the sea inside me, folded her in, like a seed, a pearl.

The accidents that can happen, Jack thinks, her hand on the curtain but not quite ready to shut out the day. Two-year-olds strangling in blind cords. Schoolchildren choking on peanuts or falling in playgrounds and never waking again. The street outside is becoming clogged with traffic, the start of the rush-hour. Lead-pollution. Asthma. A sudden dash out between cars. She shakes herself: for god's sake, get a grip, girl. After years of listening to her mother bang on about the importance of the imaginative life, *the freedom to dream, Jaqueranda, to conjure up magical beings, to become someone else, a character in a story,* she long ago decided to focus on the practical and real. This is how she is, this Jack. What will she make for the children's tea, the fair-haired girl and the nameless boy? Organic fish fingers. Peas. Yoghurts and juice.

All across the city, rain falls and day fades. Jack switches on the light and turns from the curtain to pick up toys and

95

books from the floor. She runs a hand softly over a sleepy child's hair, and when the child, goggle-eyed at the telly, brushes the hand away, she smiles and leaves them to it, going out into the kitchen to start the tea.

Then there was just one. Only one. The boy wasn't quite solid enough to last, a sweet stereotype of a child: all baby-ness and howling. In the end, it was the girl with wispy hair and bony knees that stuck it out to the end. She clung on to me, wouldn't let go, her sharp little fingers wrapped around my neck, like a chain, like a noose. Shameful of a mother to sacrifice one for another, but what choice did I have?

In the kitchen, Jack turns on the gas and gets the packet of fish fingers from the freezer. She spreads them out on a tray and puts them into the oven. She looks at the clock. Ten past five. At least an hour and a half until her husband gets home. Her daughter is tired after school and the long walk home through the rain and it's too long to wait, so maybe they'll eat here, just the two of them, Jack and her daughter, at the table, sitting calmly together in this place where nothing can happen.

There are no curtains or blinds at the kitchen window, and as she stands at the sink, running water into a pan for the peas, all she can see is the reflection. The garden has disappeared and in its place is another kitchen, projected exactly outwards from the other side of the glass. Her own face looks back at her, perfectly mirrored. My face. An ordinary woman with her hand on the tap, a straggle of fair hair falling onto her cheek. I brush it away. Behind her, behind me, is the door from the kitchen that leads into the rest of the house, into its silent spaces and hollow rooms.

Then there were none.

ALAN BEARD

# Staff Development

S OME MORNINGS ON the bus to work the dream of
the house lingers and Jack expects to end up in the
multi-roomed place, walking down corridors and stair-
cases with his parents, both dead and resurrected, and wife
and daughter and granddaughter and dog and others he
doesn't know, who all begin to jostle him with unsteady
arms and falling-off fingers. It is like the manor house he
visited last summer with Maggie. When he looks through
the window though, the glass turns to cellophane and
he's inside the doll's house he built in the shed. It sits on
a work bench. If he has to exit to avoid the scuffling, the
grabbing for him, he'll have to drop — jump — to the
chair, climb down a leg to reach the floor. Hope to hell
the cat's not around.

Instead every day, like today, Jack walks around the
security barriers, nods to some, the whistler who doesn't
stop whistling as he nods back, Ted Simms in his getting-
shiny suit, and on into the vast building that looks all
windows. On the stairs he coughs like a dog and Gregg
coming up behind slaps his back. 'All right, Jack-o? See
yer at break.'

Forgets his password again and he has to ring IT and
they are as ever sarcastic. Tut tut, Mr Bond. And they're

all of what—thirties at most—following him, his every move, tracking him across the Atlantic or the other side of the world on the web he creates from his desk. His keyboard makes him spell the simplest words wrong. Worsd. Apicrot. Grils.

At desks around him people are urging their screens on, forward, 'Come on, then.' Someone is always applying cream or lotion to hands and neck. Today Patrick is showing off nicks caused by thorn or fence, evidence of a weekend walk. Jack tries not to look at Michelle's legs as she goes past. Doesn't succeed. This man, what's his name?—can Jack have forgotten?—pads up and down, looking, sniffing with a fine long nose, for anything wrong, flaws in the air and the concrete, the desks and the people.

A birthday card is waiting to be signed on his desk: Abigail warns him to hide it before Patrick, forty at the weekend, spots it. He signs it with no note, not like others who advise the man to get drunk or to buy a red sports car, or to hibernate until it's all over.

It's getting on for forty years since they married. Is Maggie fed up with him now after all the years rolled up together? He'd first seen her as a teenager at basement dances, dancing in the crude flashing colours, time of the Beatles, the Stones, the Kinks, all those bands. She'd gone out with him, then his mate, but came back to him. The way she danced in and out of those blobby 'psychedelic' lights, her hair flicked out at the shoulders. Her face now smudged with age like his, but still soft, not many wrinkles, still her teeth pushed forward her lips, the eternal pout, from then to now. The lives they've lived together from basement disco to sheds and kitchens, via the bedroom. Chuckle, tickle, shush. He titters and his colleague beside him lifts his head from coffee never knowing how to take this older man who talks to himself a bit, quietly, and maybe he's imagining it.

Jack focuses on work. All he has to do is attend to the emails that command, finish off the files from yesterday or yesteryear, chase up the missing orders, hiding in a warehouse somewhere, acknowledge the report from the stationery subgroup. *With his comments.* He has no comments. It is simple, it is straightforward, it is staring him in the face, the C drive full of folders. All he has to do is open them and get on.

Someone is always following Jack around second-guessing and peeping into his tilted world—he has a stoop now from somewhere, the age of him, the curl of death coming up from his toes already—measuring that corner of it, where wall met skirting met floor, is it all correct, is it all in balance, is it going to withstand the wind and rain? Everybody wants to know everything: how things were between them. Man and wife, cat and dog, tree and house on a scale of one to ten, what dances they'd ever attended, which sexual position they favoured and what was their favourite soap and what made his only daughter Gemma, his only child born so late to them they'd given up, what made her up and marry that bloke, Gerard, that worthless bloke without an idea in his head or a penny in his purse. His purse. He has one. He stays home and lurks, he's done for her mentally, no violence at least, no sign, meandering on about socialism as if he knows what it is, and computer games. He sucks the energy out of every room he's in with those dog-green eyes and shoulders down. It was drugs—*chasing the dragon*, he found out—watched a programme about it; the dragon was smoke from heated black dribble across silver foil. He found evidence by the shed in the mornings. It was no good talking to her: Gemma coming off the stuff was like a drunken doll version of herself, legs on the rickety table he'd made, watching nothing on the box and her face blank. Spaced, she called it. *Dad, I'm spaced.* Static coming off her. But not any more, surely, with Jenny to look after. She's sensible that way. Is she? Takes after her mother, her clear-eyed mother. Does she? With Gerard though, there's something more. Grudge somewhere. Full of bricks and rubble. Jack had seen him pumping some poor girl in an alley, an energy found for *that*, during some party he'd come out of, music following.

A woman comes down from upstairs. 'Follow-up session,' she says. She is wearing a pinkish suit that makes Jack think of one of the figures — too small to be dolls, said Gemma at six — in the house. Stood forever by the fire-place greeting visitors. Both have a lipstick smudge in the corners of their mouths. 'Then you'll be ready to cascade.'
Jack realises after she has stood beside him smiling for a while, her eyes betraying no warmth and getting colder, as stones at night, that she wants him to get up, to offer his seat, like on the bus someone interrupting his daydream asking for tickets. He gets up and she sits down quickly like a planned, rehearsed manoeuvre, sighing a little at the strangeness of his mouse. 'It's back to front.' She clicks in her memory stick and opens the relevant program. 'I'm putting it on your desktop,' she says.
'How you get totals,' she says, 'how you get averages.' How to change screens and use other programs in conjunction. Jack says yes and I see and nods and then when it comes to showing her what he has learnt, after they have swapped places again and he is to show her the totalling function, he tries to remember the movements of her

fingers across the keyboard, he nudges a few keys and a figure turns up.

'Good, good,' she says but all he can remember now are the rings on her fingers, one gold but lacy, the red nails and the sound they made on the keys, the thin-linked silver watch, freckles on the back of her hands. The tops of her breasts, a white bra strap. The faint smell of soap around her. Imperial Leather like Maggie at home, almost silent now and he doesn't quite know why.

They're there, checking, checking, cameras turning as he passes. Even the flowers bend as he walks by. Matt Helm. He's found somewhere though, a line crossed to safety, a space where they can't see, can't follow. Down beneath fire stairs, along a corridor no one uses, a room with a broken door lock that can be latched inside. He sits for half an hour or so a day amongst discarded items, clumpy computers and screens and cabinets and broken chairs, dust springing in his nose. Clutters of broken staplers and filing trays, wire and plastic.

Not like his masterpiece at home in the shed which he still tinkers with at weekends. Like smokers with their first cigarette he inhales deeply the smell of varnish, tool metal and sawdust as he enters the shed. He might inspect a chair, almost weightless in his palm, or pore over perspective drawings. Then he gets to work, measuring (with a metal ruler so worn the figures have almost disappeared), cutting, shaping and joining. After working for an hour or so, his muscles still buzzing from the motion of plane or saw, his teeth tasting where nails had been, he stops and gazes into each room, moving furniture about until it meets with his satisfaction. He loves the way the panelled door opens with a little tug on its brass hinges. Inside it was the fireplace, windowsills and skirting boards that cost him most effort. And the stairs—they turn corners and run to landings with Chinese fret handrails. He tries to keep to the period—mini chandeliers are suspended into the downstairs rooms, little bulbs that work—but Gemma wanted a telly for them to watch, the residents and visitors, the milkman with crate and unbent legs leant on the chaise longue. The TV screen now has a picture stuck on of Emma Peel, her eyes, nose and mouth, half smiling, for him.

These days you can get kits off the internet to put together the house he'd built by himself, working out the structure from books from the library which he never visits these days but keeps saying he will and he will, maybe see the woman he brushed by in the aisles, her wave of black hair. Almost reached for it, that hair, changed his hand's direction to a shelf just in time.

He started it when Gemma was born; almost straight after he'd seen her slippery body emerge, to Maggie's final scream, anointed in oily colours. That night, when they finally chased him out of the ward, her smell still all about him, he started on the plans, smiling, the smile staying for days. And finished—never quite finished. There is always something to change: classier cutlery for the table; some new figure to see if it fits; a miniature Picasso, completely wrong time but what the hell, from his blue period, to hang.

In the toilet washing his hands Gregg catches him and says straight away how so and so botched up a job and still got promoted. 'Doesn't that stink?' He leans into Jack, can see a gold filling in a back tooth, feel the ginger breath on him. Gregg always knows, is keeping tabs: the down-sizing, the rumours, the temporary staff they're going to bring in, who's fucking who.

'Always the same crowd. Round each other's houses for cheese and wine.' Gregg whines like a wolf, his head back. 'They all know too much, know where all the bodies are buried.' He turns, unzipping, to the urinal but carries on over his shoulder.

'That's the hold Ted Simms and Jackie Ripple have over them all. You know they're *liaising*, don't you. Fucked in that stall there'—he nods to the side of him and Jack nods back at him in the mirror. 'Heard 'em, must have been a week ago, recognised his cough and her . . . little cry. Aahh, ah.' Gregg is pissing merrily now. 'I looked under the door but she'd pulled her feet up. Probably sat on his lap.' He zips up and turns. 'Fucking bastards. If I were you, Jack, I'd kick up hell the way they're treating you, you've been here longer than all of them put together. These warnings they're giving you are a disgrace.'

Jack has forgotten the warnings they've given him.

He could make it to his daughter's street and back in the lunch hour, just to say hello, spot how she's doing with Jenny, remember how wearing five-, six-year-olds can be, but fun too. Talk about getting the doll's house ready for Jenny to play with when they visit, new things, a miniature computer maybe in the corner of a room, take out something, the bookcase because the books weren't real looking, weren't separate things. Can't really bring it to her, would have to dismantle the shed to get it out. It wouldn't fit through door or window. Maggie was not surprised to hear of that. He would always cock something up, she reckoned. Look at that wonky table in their front room. He'd never been able to adapt his skills to their home, gave up after that one attempt, the larger scale defeated him. 'Can't you unglue, unscrew it, take it out in bits?' He couldn't bear the thought of that.

Jenny is the same age as when Gemma was formally presented with it, a blue ribbon wrapped round, a bow tied between the chimneys. He continued to work on it though, from her sixth to her sixteenth, sometimes while she was there having little conversations between the characters, the figures he bought for her, an odd assortment, tended to be firemen or police or film stars then, Clint Eastwood in a dining room demanding his beans on toast. Even in her teens, fourteen, fifteen, she'd come and move them about, a refuge from bullies, a gang who called her names and wrote bitch and worse about her on walls. He'd try and talk to her about them, the names called, the hurt, while sanding a door, or screwing in a hinge with a spectacle screwdriver, such close beady-eyed work, but she didn't want to say. Looking across to her though, her pinched face coming into focus, he thought she was glad of him there. Within arm's reach.

Then it was short skirts, boys, drugs. Those days of nothing doing, a tired insolence, and then the pregnancy sprung on them all. Until recently the house unused, not played with, or upgraded or changed while Gemma brought up Jenny. She left for a starter home, one storey with a mezzanine, a balconied bedroom, still there with her non-starter husband. Gerard works on and off but never accumulates enough to leave. Maggie and Jack were together then, united in their help and time spent with Gemma, with Jenny shared between each other's arms. Baby sick back in their lives. Songs sung and stories told about wolves and pigs. Tolerating Gerard. 'Can't pin that bloke down,' Maggie would say after an hour of smiling at him. Sex returned, briefly, like a flare in the night. Before the cat reclaimed her lap.

And now, on visits, Jenny found granddad's secret house in the shed, and tried all the doors and peered into rooms and got her big childish fingers into his rooms and the figures were once again moved about. He didn't mind, not even the inevitable breakages, a chandelier, a chair leg. He was there with her, sniggering over her fat teacher with her, asking about her dad, does he help her mum, does he read to her?

At lunch on his way there Jack stops to buy a cake, a present for Gemma and Jenny, not for Gerard, Slim Jim, man about the sofa. He has forgotten supermarket eti-quette, how you have to respond quickly to movement, shift with the queue or get a trolley in your thigh. And then there is the point where he thinks he doesn't have enough money and searches pockets he never knew he had, and the man behind tuts in smoker's throat until he finds the coins and counts them out and leaves carrying the cake out in front of him, can't have it on its side, its filling would come out.

Jack reaches the corner of her street and sees Gemma leave, go the other way, maybe he could shout but it's a long street, she's quite a way down so he tries to run with the cake box in front of him, but gives in and stops outside her house, he is almost looking down on its one boxy storey, seeing her ahead disappear. Thin as her bloke with long black hair, always naturally curly, he'd brushed it until sleek for years. She looks small now, pulled along by a little dog, smaller than when she was a kid somehow. Dog shit everywhere on their strip of lawn below. He is taken over by the vision of her moments before — turn from the door, tug the lead, her dark jeans, her knee turns, away, that movement, her turning from the door seconds before, takes over him. He stands still in the street, someone bringing out a black rubbish bag, a car reversing into a space beside him, outside her house with the cake box held before him. Half way down a street curving to the left, blurred movement around him, like it is raining all around, at the edge of the space he creates. He can't move, he can't go on.

A woman wheels a pushchair past, the half-asleep baby wakes and points at him, a dog comes up and sniffs the back of his knees and he stands like a horse sometimes stands in a field, not moving an eyelid.

And then there he is, Gerard, the left-wing man, Jack and Maggie are on that side too, but he takes it too far. Shoot the royal family and cigar smokers, redistribute wealth into his pockets. There was the night of the party when Jack caught him with another woman, he'd come out because he was drunk and needed air and made the mistake of walking a bit. His son-in-law's back, his uncovered arse going back and forth and the girl lifting her skirt up, sat on a wall, down an alley. He knew the girl, friend of Gemma's, she was turning the other way with the thrusts but then her head turned round to see Jack. Didn't stop, just looked with eyes like buttons. Later he'd said to Gerard, returning to the party, he'd waited for him, 'Why don't you piss off, run away with her?' And he'd never told Maggie, he didn't know why, he didn't want her to think about it. Or Gemma.

Here he is, not pissed off with anyone, not properly dressed, smelling of days indoors taking Gemma's and Jenny's and not his present from Jack's hands and talking into his face but Jack can't seem to respond to the cocked eyebrow and the shrugged shoulders of him turning away, except to say when he reaches the door down below him 'I spose she's out getting your drugs for you?' and he goes in to the little house with the cake balanced on one hand.

He is late back; he goes down to his room again, under the stairs. It was on his third visit he masturbated. Sat on the wheeled chair, pushed up in a corner to stop it rolling. Thinking of the good days with his wife that fell upon them not at once, but after a struggle, misunderstandings. When she didn't get pregnant and they'd thought she never would, sex — for a while — became easy, slow and messy, but no rushing to clear it up as before, an acceptance.

He also thinks, now, of Jackie Ripple, her flesh like ice cream to go with her name, leaving lipstick on him, all over him.

The sperm went, goes now, into the drawer of an old desk nearby, fingers clamped until he gets in the right position to let go, splash against the inside wood, whacking the dribble in. How nice to slide it shut after, the tissues he always carries or if forgot paper from the gents', now applied. Stood, stands, the king of his room, anyone who came in, comes in, would see a man exalted. As if his child had become rich and famous, safe. And happy, happier than any film star on a set. But also everything is pushed away, there is only him, having come, in a room beneath the stairs.

Jack is called into the boss's office, maybe he's been seen below, maybe someone's been in there and spotted something, a drawing he'd scribbled on wood, his pen dropped nearby. He passes the model under glass: a cleaner, whiter, blanker building, figures outside, mini-trees, a bus stop with a single-decker pulling away. The future.

There is a woman present who sits between them and looks from one to the other. His boss is telling him how appreciated he is, overall, but there were certain things, certain worries. Jack thinks he'll get on with everything now, he'll finish off those files, those training portfolios, he'll be an ace of the Supplies Department. An exemplar.

How would it be if everyone came up and told him how good he was at his job and how loved by everyone he was, didn't he know it, he was a *fixture*, been here from the start, when the company set up here, blimey been here pre-computers, he was the permanent figure in the house always doing the dishes.

His boss's moustache seems a little wonky and Jack wants to ask if he's fucking Jackie Ripple in the gents' too much to concentrate on his appearance, or wouldn't that make you more meticulous with it, trimming the ends to point at her breasts while you're doing it. Gregg is convinced that Ted Boss is wearing a wig and Jack tries not to look to check at the hairline that does seem a little too neat, a little too perfect. No, she'd pull it off during all that activity and laugh, or maybe she didn't mind.

Everything he says, bewigged fucker of perfect wobbling flesh — just jealous — the man with notes in his hand, his *line manager*, begins or contains 'just'.

'Just that you were seen running, stopping and then running again. Back the way you came.'

'We're just a little concerned now. Progress on your objectives has been slow, Erica tells me.'

'Well, we'll just see how it goes. No need for a big fuss just yet.'

Ted Shatmachine's eyes seem to have bits in them. Little red bits like bits of match-heads. The woman seems to be in a pool of grey air, when she speaks the grey air shudders as if plucked, although she doesn't speak much, she turns mainly to fucker — perhaps she wants a fuck too, perhaps they're all going off to the toilet together to have a merry threesome — and nods him on or slightly shakes her head or raises an eyebrow at what he is saying.

Jack is reminded of his forthcoming IPR, the goals he'd set in the last one, how far had he got? Were they

achievable, did the training help? He has to break out
of silo thinking. He hasn't completely blown it, he can
tell from the smiles, the crease of his boss's mouth only
seeming to one side because of the little scar on the other.
Had he had a childhood accident? Is the window coming
undone behind him? His boss moves back and forth in
his chair, back and forth and Jack listens to the squeaks.

There is a fair chance everything will turn out just
fine. Let's make this department the envy of the Western
world. Everybody with the correct supplies at the correct
time. Not a pencil out of place. He just has to watch his
footsteps, that's all, see where they go and stop them if
need be. Was that clear? The square of the room was
rounding out, beginning to spin, like someone has started
to play some daft rock and roll like 'Rosalyn' by the Pretty
Things, not the Bowie cover version, what if Maggie had
gone for Richard, his rival in the youth club days, he
would sing different songs. All he has to do is watch where
he's stepping, none of the dog shit in his daughter's house,
none of that. Pass on his recent training. Let's see him
back on track. That's the way, don't you see?

Gregg catches him on his way back to his desk. What
were the ins and outs, what had Cocky Ted said now,
should they get the unions in? We should just let them all
have it, he machine-guns everyone coming down the corridor, ack–ack–ack, tell them everything we know, hey?
He taps his nose at Jack.

He's only been at his terminal minutes when she arrives,
it's not the same woman as this morning, she smells different: Sure deodorant, Jack reckons, tuna for lunch. Same
hair as his daughter, except thicker, richer, cleaner like
Gemma's was, pre-Gerard days, fuller in figure too. Stood
by the side of him as bright as strip-lighting talking.

More training, thinks Jack, when she mentions the program he'd been shown this morning, and he knows exactly where it is on the screen, it's on the desktop, he can go right there and double click it into life. Ping. 'There you are,' he says. 'Was there extra? Add-ons?' He'd heard someone say that recently.

She looks up and down the room, confused. Her stance, why is he noticing everyone's stance: his daughter in the street turning, Maggie standing by the door each morning to see him out, peck on the cheek, Gerard's head hung before him, get his nose into everything first, this girl as if about to flee and her lips pink with a gloss on them, he appreciates the gloss, her lips try to say something but decide not to. Then he realises what her stance is trying to say, is telling him, he is supposed to train *her*. She is waiting to be trained, she is taking her first steps in office work, her career there may be forever like his, every day she'll come on the bus or drive or maybe she'll get out, she'll escape, she'll drop to the floor and fight off the bothersome cat, its claws and teeth, easily.

He gets off his chair again, to offer it to her. While she settles and moves his strange mouse he goes to the window, hello hello, Abigail and Patrick, I nod nod nod you and he tries to open the window beyond the suicide bar and whistles down at the security men sat in their little booth near where the bus drops him each morning, he thinks of Jesus in a hay barn, Hayley Mills and lemonade. He comes back to her, looking over her shoulder at him, along the burning pavements of his youth, the wasps and the bees, the land all blue.

How like his daughter she is, at one point in her life, how she might have been. How she could be loose-limbed and carefree, if she'd ditched Gerard, if she'd escaped. If she'd never met him. This new girl in his chair was Janette, she'd said, and gave him her hand, didn't she, didn't she have the cold quiet fingers reaching for him in the dream, on the bus, the ticket collector, the queue of zombies wanting more. Janette's eyes reflected all the sex she'd had and all the sex to come. Her eyes said he would be replaced, he would be gone soon. Like Gregg said, after thirty years' service, nearly. How the office would be without him, how it was already without him, once thought indispensable, everybody's pal, her eyes told him all this.

'What it does', he says, eyeing the screen, 'is eat numbers. Nombres. Numbbums.' Janette nods, glad to talk about the program at last, after all the waiting. He leans over, so close to her hair and neck, to use the mouse and clicks on a figure in a box.

'It eats numbers,' Jack says, 'and has a big fat brelly.' He rubs his stomach like he is telling Gemma *Red Riding Hood* when she is old enough to be scared, to respond. 'Then spews them out, *regurgitates* them. We should serve them up, sever them up, on *little tiny* plates' — he shows how big with the tips of finger and thumb — 'covered in roses to the royalty here, the bosses and ladies of the manor, don't you think?'

He says the hub, where they should go, to see the engine and wave at the driver, is downstairs. He'll take her there, would she care to stand up and follow him. He grasps her shoulder, it fits like a socket joint in his palm, he can feel her clavicle, her flesh and bra strap beneath white blouse, the warmth and shiver in it, the hardness of bone, her black hair nylon strands against the back of his fingers. He has it in mind they will both squeeze into that crowded small room he has made and he'll show her the furniture, the broken wheeled chair she could sit on

and he'll bark out his orders like Clint Eastwood, only it
will all be sexual.

# The Rental Heart

THE DAY AFTER I met Grace—her pierced little mouth, her shitkicker boots, her hands as small as goosebumps writing numbers on my palm. The day after I met her, I went to the heart rental place.

I hadn't rented in years, and doubted they would have my preferred model. The window display was different, the hearts sleeker and shinier than I remembered. The first time I had rented it was considered high-tech to have the cogs tucked away; now they were as smooth and seamless as a stone. Some of the new hearts had extras I'd never seen, like timers and standby buttons and customised beating patterns.

That made me think about Grace, her ear pressed to my sternum, listening to the morse code of her name, and my own heart started to creep up my throat so I swallowed it down and went into the shop.

An hour later I was swallowing lunch and trying to read the instruction leaflet. They made it seem so complicated but it wasn't really. The hearts just clipped in, and as long as you remembered to close yourself up tightly then they could tick away for years. Decades, probably. The problems came when the hearts got old and scratched:

shreds of the past got caught in the dents, and they're tricky to rinse out. Even a wire brush won't do it.

But the man in the rental place had assured me that this one was factory-fresh, clean as a kitten's tongue. Those heart rental guys always lied, but I could tell by the heart's coppery sheen that it hadn't been broken yet.

I remembered perfectly well how to fit the heart, but I still read the leaflet to the end as a distraction. A way to not think about how Grace looked when she bit her lip, when she wrote the curls of her number. How she would look later tonight, when she. When we.

It was very important that I fit the heart before that happened.

Ten years ago, first heart. Jacob was as solid and golden as a tilled field, and our love was going to last for ever, which at our age meant six months. Every time Jacob touched me, I felt my heart thud wetly against my lungs. When I watched him sleep, I felt it clawing up my oesophagus. Sometimes it was hard to speak from the wet weight of it sitting at the base of my tongue, but I would just smile and wait for him to start talking again.

The more I loved him the heavier my heart felt, until I was walking around with my back bent and my knees cracking from the weight of it. When Jacob left, I felt my heart shatter like a shotgun pellet, shards lodging in my guts. I had to drink every night to wash the shards out. I had to.

A year later I met Anna. She was dreadlocked, green eyed, full of verbs. She smelled of rain and revolution. I fell.

But the parts of me that I wanted to give to Anna were long gone, down the gutters of the city, mixed with the chemicals of forgetting. Those shards had dissolved, washed away for ever, and there was not enough left that was worth giving. The edges of my heart were jagged now and I did not want to feel those rough edges climbing my throat; I did not love her enough to cough blood. I kept what was left of me close, tucked under the long soft coils of my intestines where Anna wouldn't see.

One night, still throbbing, Anna opened her chest. Her heart nestled, a perfect curl of clockwork.

*This is how,* she said.

I could hear its tick against the soft embrace of her lungs, and I bent close to her to smell its metallic sharpness. I wanted.

The next day she took me to the heart rental place. I spent a long time pressing my palms against the polished metal until I found one that felt warm against my skin. I made sure that the sharp edges of the cogs were tucked inwards, kept safe from the just-healed rawness of my throat.

Back at Anna's, she unwrapped the plastic, fitted the heart, closed my chest, took me to bed. Later I watched her sleep and loved her with every cog of my heart.

When Anna ran off with my best friend I took the heart back to the rental place. Nothing choked or shattered or weighed me down. It looked just as sleekshiny as when I had first taken it out of the wrapping, and the rental guy gave me my full deposit back. I deleted Anna's phone number and went out for dinner.

The next year, when I met Will, I knew what to do. The heart this time was smaller, more compact, and it clipped into place easily. Technology moves fast.

Will taught me about Boudicea, the golden section, musical intervals, Middle English. I soaked him up like I was cotton wool.

Sometimes, pre-dawn, I would sneak into the bathroom and open myself to the mirror. The heart reflected

Will back at me, secure in its mechanics. I would unclip it, watch it tick in my fist. I would put it back before sliding into Will's arms.

On our first holiday, I beeped through the airport barriers. I showed my heart and was waved on. It wasn't until the plane was taxiing that I realised Will had not beeped. I spent the whole flight wire-jawed with my paperback open to page one, unable to stop thinking about the contents of Will's chest. We never mentioned it; I could not stand to think of his chest cavity all full of wet red flesh.

When I left Will, I returned the heart again. I couldn't sleep for the thought of his heart, shot into shards, sticking in his guts, scratching up his gullet.

After that I rented hearts for Michael, and Rose, and Genevieve. They taught me about Heisenberg's Uncertainty Principle and how to look after a sausage dog. They smelled of petrol and hair oil and sawdust and honeysuckle.

After a while, the heart rental guy started to greet me by name. He gave me a bulk discount and I got invited to his Christmas party. Soon I found that halfway between sleeping and waking, the glint of the rental guy's gold incisor would flicker at the corners of my eyes. I wondered if he licked the hearts before renting them to me, so molecules of him would be caught down in some tiny hidden cog, merging into my insides.

The glint of the rental guy in my dreams started to make me uncomfortable, so I switched to a new rental place. There were plenty to choose from, and I preferred the ones that didn't gleam their teeth at me. They never gave me back my security deposits, but always kept their stares on the scratched glass counter when I returned the hearts. Their downturned eyes were more important than the shine of coins.

I got older, the hearts got smaller. After Genevieve I moved away for a while, to an island where I knew no-one and nothing, not even the language. I lived alone. I did not look anyone in the eye; I did not need to rent a heart. My empty chest made it easy to breathe, and I filled my lungs with the sharp air of the sea. I stayed there for a year.

Back in the city, back in the world. Among words and faces I knew. One night, many drinks, and Grace's number scrawled tiny on my skin. Then the downturned gaze, the scratched glass counter. The sleekshiny new heart.

I swallowed the rest of my lunch and went home to fit the heart.

Three years later, autumn afternoon, curled on the couch with newsprint on my fingers and Grace's dozing hair in my lap. I stuttered on a small notice in the corner of the page: *Product recall: Heart Model #345-27J. Defective.*

I pressed my hand—the hand holding the dark length of Grace's hair—against my chest. I hadn't opened myself in years, trusting the tick of the heart. I'd kept it for so long that I knew I'd have lost my deposit, but I hadn't wanted to return it, to lose the image of Grace coiled in the centre of it. I'd forgotten the face of the rental guy; had forgotten the warm weight of a new heart in my palm.

I slid out from under Grace. She mumbled half-awake, then quietened when I slipped a cushion in under the heat of her skull. I tiptoed into the bathroom and opened the rusted hinges of my chest.

The heart was dusty and tarnished and utterly empty. In the centre of it was no picture of Grace, no strands of her hair, no shine of memories, no declarations. The rusting metal squealed when I pulled it out.

PHILIP LANGESKOV

# Notes on a Love Story[1]

IN THE EVENING — it was Friday — he picked her up in the car from the back entrance on Jermyn Street. The traffic was heavy and they moved slowly round St James's, cars edging forward, bumper to bumper. On Piccadilly, hotel porters ran this way and that, flagging down taxis, and pushing luggage trolleys along the pavement. It was October, just before the equinox, and the last rays of sun glowed on the curves of the buses idling alongside.

As Sam drove, Sarah crouched down in the footwell and changed out of her uniform, her arms at unusual angles.

'I've got something to show you,' he said.

That morning, he had received his copy of the *Paris Review*. It was the first story he'd had published. When it arrived, he stood in the kitchen, at the breakfast counter, staring at the brown paper package. He must have read it five or six times, finding it hard to believe it was his. The font, the layout, the positioning, placed between two poems, one by Jorie Graham,[2] another by Paul Muldoon, contrived to distance it from the story he had laboured over for months in the back bedroom. But there it was, his name, Sam Longwood, in sixteen-point Cambria. Just to be sure, he checked the contents page. *Sleeping Dogs*, by Sam Longwood, page 155. The editor had put a note in the package. *We are pleased to have it. Plimpton.*[3]

He handed the magazine to her as they drove down Whitechapel Road.

'My God,' she said. 'Is this it?'

She read it as they sat in a tailback near Gants Hill. He watched her as she read, his right hand resting on the steering wheel. She pored over every word, her hair slipping down from behind her ear. When she finished, she looked up. She edged across in her seat, put her arms around his neck and hung there. He could smell her perfume, the one he sniffed, quietly, in the bathroom when she was away on trips.

'I'm so proud of you.'

They arrived late, and had to park at the edge of the estuary,[4] in the dark, and wait for the tide to recede. Three hours in the cold and then, stone by stone, the causeway[5] emerged. The house,[6] an eccentric, rambling, wooden construction, rose like a lighthouse at the north-eastern tip of the island.[7]

'What shall we do? Eat, walk? Walk, eat?'

'Walk, then eat.'

It was nearly midnight when they set off, walking briskly by the light of the moon, inhaling the brackish air of the salt marsh. The path led inland to the south-west and then hooked east towards the raised bank of an earthen sea wall. As they approached, across an open field, they heard the noise.

'What's that?' said Sarah.

'I don't know.'

'Come on. Run.'

She set off, the material of her padded coat swishing,

her breath puffing out and trailing in the air behind her. By the time they reached the foot of the bank he had overhauled her. The noises—whatever they were—grew and grew. They climbed together, leaning into the slope, pulling themselves up, grabbing clumps of thick, brittle grass. At the top, they saw.

Geese. Thousands upon thousands of brent geese.[8] They floated, moving with the gentle ebb of the estuary, bobbing amid the moon, the stars, the clear sky, and the tracks of the Milky Way, which lay reflected silver-white on the black surface of the water. And the noise. Deafening. It rose into the air, turning and twisting. They had heard bird call before, many times, but this was different. These birds—like an army gathering on a hillside in the grey dawn before battle—were talking to each other, shouting and shrieking across the flats, their voices rebounding off the water and quivering in the reeds.

'My God,' she said. 'Look at them.'

And then.

'Look. Look up there.'

'Where?'

'There.'

He raised his arm and pointed. A thick blanket of cloud—like a wall, or a wave, or a mountain range—was being drawn across the sky. It raced towards them, the white wisps of its towering front edge swirling and roiling. It seemed close enough to touch. One by one, the stars were gathered in, the acres of clear sky, the moon.

He crouched down to get the camera out of his bag.

'No,' she said, lifting her hand. 'Just watch.'[9]

On it rolled, the bank of cloud, seeming to gather pace as it passed over the wrecked wooden hulk of a Thames barge,[10] its rotting mast listing to port. And then it was above them, engulfing the air; something monstrous, immense, unparalleled. A ripple broke the surface of the water and the geese—the thousands of geese—rose politely and then fell again, one after another. Sarah and Sam stood on the bank, their eyes turned skywards and their mouths open, like witnesses to a rare and ancient ceremony—an initiation rite, a sacrifice. For a moment, there was quiet and it seemed as if something grand and important, a secret as old as the world itself, was being whispered to them. They clung to one another, dwarfed, as the clouds rolled on and on, away over the estuary and out to the open sea.

And then, a honk, then another and then another. The geese. Their shouts had resumed.

## THE END.[11]

### ENDNOTES

[1]  'All stories are love stories.' So begins Robert McLiam Wilson's 1996 novel, *Eureka Street*. It is a spare and haunting beginning but if you tweak it a bit, if you strip the line down further, to its barest essentials—subject-verb-object—you will find a formulation that might be etched on a primary-school wall: stories love stories.

Around the time Wilson's novel was being published, another novelist and short-story writer, Neil Davidson, was recovering in hospital after a nervous breakdown brought on by difficulties he experienced in completing his third novel, *The Hallucination* (see below). Alex Johns, of the *Observer*, was interviewing him for an article on the consequences of creativity. The interview took place on a Saturday morning in August 1996. I was in the room.

The television, on a wall bracket, was tuned to the third Test Match between England and Pakistan, taking place at the Oval. Having been asked a question, Neil would turn his attention to the unfolding action on the screen. For minutes at a time, he would appear to become lost in the movement of the white-flannelled players. Then, without taking his eyes off the game, Neil would lift his head, tilt it slightly to the left and respond. One question had been to do with the pressure to produce. This is how Neil replied:

'Writing a novel,' he said, 'is like a love affair. You can't look for one. You have to wait for it to happen.'

Shortly after noon, I left them to it and returned to my flat just off Borough High Street, where I settled down to my Saturday stint of three hours' writing. Against Neil's advice, I was working on something that I had actively sought out: a novel, inspired by Dostoevsky's *The Adolescent*, about two middle-class teenagers who commit a gruesome murder. I had reached that point when the suspicion that a certain project is flawed crystallises into unarguable fact. By the end of the three hours I had resolved, finally, to abandon the venture. At the time, still an apprentice, I had to fit my writing around a full-time job. Consequently, not only was I beset by feelings of inadequacy at my inability to realise the fictional world I had set out to create, I was also angry with myself for wasting so many hours on something so obviously unmanageable. Orhan Pamuk, the Turkish Nobel Laureate, writes powerfully about the blackness that descends when a writer cannot write:

'Let me explain what I feel on a day when I've not written well, if I'm not lost in a book. First, the world changes before my eyes: it becomes unbearable, abominable . . . during these dark moments, I feel as if there is no line between life and death.'

That is how I felt that afternoon, as if there was no line between life and death. I spent the remainder of the day in a daze, ironing shirts and preparing to go to a party being held that evening to celebrate the wedding anniversary of some old friends. I didn't want to go — the last thing I wanted was company — but I had been best man at the wedding. I had to go. I forced myself out of the door and, in an attempt to clear my head, walked over the bridge as far as Shoreditch High Street, where I caught the bus, the 277.

Sarah was standing in the garden, towards the back, talking to a friend of mine.

She came back to mine that evening. Neither of us expected that. It was nearly dawn by the time she fell asleep; I listened for the change in her breathing. When I was certain she was sleeping, I lifted her arm from my chest and crept to the back bedroom, switched on my computer and began to write.

The story had come to me, fully formed, earlier that evening as we stood under the trees. 'How It Will End'. I imagined it all, from its magical beginning at a party in North London to its shattering conclusion, the force of which would reverberate week after week, month after month, year after year. It was as if a space had opened up in front of me, a bubble that stretched from the present, to the future, and then back again. I wasn't even thinking about stories and yet there it was, complete. WG Sebald is good on how things can come to us when we least expect them: 'Every writer knows that sometimes the best ideas come to you while you are reading something else, say, about Bismarck, and then suddenly, somewhere between the lines, your head starts drifting, and you arrive at the ideas that you need.'

I knew that I had to get something down, even if it was just the frame, the shape. I wrote until ten and then slipped into bed and curled against the warmth of Sarah's back.

I didn't tell Sarah about the story. It would have been too hard to explain. What I did do, the next afternoon, was send a postcard to Neil in his hospital bed.

*Neil,* I wrote. *I was interested to hear you say, yesterday, that a novel cannot be looked for. I agree with you, but last night, at that party, I met someone, and, in my giddiness, I'd like to turn your line around. A love affair is like writing a novel. You can't look for one. You have to wait for it to happen.*

2.  American poet, 1950–present. Attracted controversy when, in 1999, in her capacity as judge of the Contemporary Poetry Prize at the University of Georgia, she awarded first place to the South African poet Peter Sacks. Not only did Graham know Sacks, she would, in 2000, become his wife. The things (allegedly) we do for love.

3.  George Plimpton, 1927–2003. American writer and fabled editor of the *Paris Review* — second only to William Maxwell (Fiction Editor, the *New Yorker*, 1936–75), in terms of his encouragement of young writers, especially those who practise the art of short fiction.

4.  The Blackwater Estuary lies at the mouth of the River Blackwater, in the county of Essex in south-east England. It is among the most productive estuaries in the United Kingdom, providing a protected habitat to a wealth of seabirds, including the Ringed Plover (*Charadrius hiaticula*), the Black-tailed Godwit (*Limosa limosa islandica*) and the Common Shelduck (*Tadorna tadorna*). It is also home to the Colchester Native, one of the most sought after varieties of oyster in the world.

In the autumn of 2001, Sarah and I spent a week in Paris. I had been invited by Penelope Fletcher Le Masson — the Canadian owner of The Yellow Flower bookshop — to take part in a literary festival.

The bookshop, named after the William Carlos Williams poem, was at that time on Rue Clovis opposite the entrance to the Lycée Henri IV, the school from which Marthe collects the narrator of Radiguet's *Le Diable au Corps* and takes him shopping for furniture. It is the moment in the novel at which we realise they will fall in love.

I read two stories that night. It was the first time Sarah had seen me read. She sat at the back. It is the best reading I have ever given.

Afterwards, we walked in a loop through the Marais, back across the Pont des Arts and into Saint-Germain-des-Prés. It was a Saturday night and the terraces of the haunted cafés were full. Penelope had booked us a table at Le Petit Zinc, a restaurant on Rue Saint-Benoît in the 6th, and one of the finest seafood restaurants in the city. On arrival we were greeted by a blackboard on which was written:

*Vient d'arriver! Huîtres indigènes de Colchester*

The restaurant was packed.

Incidentally, that week we stayed at the Hotel d'Angleterre on Rue Jacob. Formerly the British Embassy, it was where the Treaty of Paris, ending the American War of Independence, was signed in 1783. One hundred and thirty-eight years later a couple, newly married and very much in love, arrived from Oak Park, Chicago. The couple were the Hemingways, Ernest and Hadley. While in residence, in Room 11, Ernest wrote 'The End of Something', that cruel, cold story about the end of a love affair.

5.  The causeway connects Northey Island (see below) to the mainland and is believed to be the site of the Battle of Maldon, which took place on 10 August 991. A band of Viking raiders, under the leadership of the fearsome Anlaf, fought with an Anglo-Saxon force led by Earl Byrhtnoth. The day before the battle, Anlaf offered to withdraw in return for a payment of Danegeld. Byrhtnoth, a proud man, rejected the offer, spitting at Anlaf's feet. The next afternoon — the morning had been spent waiting for the tide to recede, just as Sarah and I had waited that evening — battle was joined on the causeway. It was a bloody fight. Byrhtnoth was mortally wounded by a poisoned spear and although his men fought bravely they were eventually overrun.

    After the battle it is said that Byrhtnoth's retainers carried his body home to his wife, Ælfflæd, who stitched a tapestry memorialising her husband's deeds.

    The battle was recorded in an epic poem composed sometime around 995. The only extant copy of the manuscript was lost in the nineteenth century; an eighteenth-century copy, the Elphinstone Transcription, resides at the British Library. One of the most celebrated lines from the poem is this, attributed to Byrhtwold the Aged: 'Heart must be braver, courage the bolder, mood the stouter, even as our strength grows less.'

6.  The house was designed and built in the 1920s by Norman Hart (1872–1967). Hart, a distinguished British journalist, academic and diplomat, is the subject of Neil Davidson's unpublished *The Hallucination*. Now a mere footnote to history, Hart was a significant figure in world affairs for almost fifty years. He was the author of over forty books, most notably *The Grand Hallucination* (1910), in which he developed his controversial theory on power. The theory was tremendously influential and the book, translated into over twenty-five languages, sold over 2 million copies.

    Davidson's novel covers none of this, preferring instead another hallucination: the story of Hart's love for Ellen Hawthatch. Hawthatch was the daughter of Robert Settle Hawthatch III, proprietor of the *St Louis Globe-Democrat*, for whom Hart worked as a reporter from 1894–8. The couple fell deeply in love and, in 1897, Hart asked Ellen to marry him. She accepted. However, Hart, a man ascetic both in manner and countenance, broke the engagement in 1898, fearing his reserved nature would never allow the couple — and particularly the free-spirited

Ellen—to be truly happy. Despite the entreaties of her father he refused to change his mind and fled back to Europe, to Paris, where he acted as correspondent for a number of American newspapers, covering, among other things, the progress of the Dreyfus case.

Hart threw himself into his work, but he could not banish Ellen from his mind. He wanted to renounce his decision, or for her to tell him that she could not live without him. In 1901 he returned to America with the intention of throwing himself on her mercy. On the boat from Southampton he met an acquaintance of her father; the summer before, Ellen had married someone else. Hart was shattered. On arrival in New York, he transferred his trunk to the next outbound steamer and returned to Europe.

Hart never forgot Ellen. He dedicated all his books to her and, upon his death sixty-six years later, his family were outraged to discover that she was named as the sole beneficiary of his will.

I told this story to Sarah on the night of our stay on Northey, in the house now owned by David and Sarah Ryan, direct descendants of the Hawthatches of St Louis. The house is still there, and can be rented for weekends or longer. It is the perfect spot for bird-watchers, for writers and for lovers.

7. Northey Island, located in the Blackwater Estuary. The night before the Battle of Maldon (see above), Anlaf's men camped on Northey. They ate a supper of Colchester Natives, dredged from the bed of the estuary using wooden grabs not unlike wide brooms.

8. Brent geese (*Branta bernicla*) can be divided into two separate strands: dark-bellied (*Branta bernicla bernicla*) and pale-bellied (*Branta bernicla hrota*). Pale-bellied brents breed mostly in Canada (especially the Queen Elizabeth Islands) and the south-western flank of Greenland, and spend the winter in the milder climate on the western coast of Ireland; dark-bellied brents breed in the Arctic tundra of Northern Russia and winter on the estuaries of south-east England. The Blackwater Estuary provides a winter residence to approximately 50 per cent of the global population of dark-bellied brents. They arrive in England from their Arctic breeding grounds from mid-October to early November, where they remain until the following spring. More like humans than swans, the notion of a single life partner—of enduring love—is an ideal rather than a constantly achieved reality for brent geese.

9. Photography played a large part in our relationship. Sarah was the more accomplished, and I always deferred to her judgement on composition, aperture speed and other technical considerations.

Early in our relationship we spent a week in New York. We were in the first flush; everything we tried came off. The weather, for example, was perfect. We took a risk, travelling in late March. The week before our arrival—we both checked the weather forecast with something bordering on obsession—the eastern seaboard of the United States was in the grip of a cold snap: snow, ice, plummeting temperatures. We prepared to pack polo necks, winter coats, even face masks—we had heard about the winds that whipped down the avenues and cross streets. Then, perhaps even while we were in the air, spring broke. The snow melted, the ice disappeared and the thermometer soared. By the time we landed, it was mid-teens and shirt-sleeve order.

One morning—it was a Thursday—we went to a Diane Arbus retrospective at the Whitney. It was a wonderful show. As well as showing much of her work, the exhibition focused on her working method, how she would surround herself with collages of things that interested her: photographs, images, sketches, newspaper cuttings, menu cards, quotations. Some of the quotations were etched on the wall. This, from Plato's *Euthyphro*, was one: 'A thing is not seen because it is visible, but conversely, visible because it is seen.'

That afternoon, walking through Washington Square—we walked everywhere on that trip, traversing Manhattan from east to west, from north to south—I started taking pictures. She was wearing a red jacket, the collar turned up to her chin. The film was black and white—Sarah's idea, she had been taking some shots of the wires of the Brooklyn Bridge—and as I crouched, Sarah turned in the middle of the square. She looked over her shoulder, eyes like Sophia Loren.

'Hang on,' I said. 'Hold that pose.'

I had seen something.

Weeks later, when we picked up the photographs from Joe's Basement in Soho, we discovered that what I had seen had—as Plato said it would—become visible. It was love that I had seen: love in her eyes, in the smoothness of her skin and in the way her hair—the brown made black by the film—was caught, flung out, almost horizontal, as she turned to look at me. For years, that photograph hung on the wall in our bedroom, her eyes a seen and visible reminder that in each other we had found something rare, something precious.

10. The barge is *The Mistley*. She is still there, stranded, rotting away on the salt marsh, her timbers turning to mud, fibre by fibre. Thames barge no. 91336, she was built in 1891 by the noted shipwrights John and Herbert Cann of Harwich. She was bought by Samuel Horatio Horlock, who employed her to carry wheat and other grain from his loading station at Mistley, Essex, to the East India docks on the Thames, from where the wheat was distributed and carried to all corners of the British Empire. No one can recall how she ran aground. Today, she is commemorated in the name of the Mistley Barge, a public house in Maldon. The proprietors of the pub, Professor David Marsh (University of Essex) and his wife, Amanda, met and fell in love while part of a team conducting a survey of the wreck in 1987.

11. It ended for us in 2003. It happened suddenly. I suppose I had always

known that it would. For seven years we had been in love. Although we never married, we did once come close.

We were on holiday, a driving tour that had taken us from London, through France, and along the Côte d'Azur. We drove into Italy, on a road that swept, on stilts and in tunnels, through the foothills of the Ligurian Riviera. We were about an hour past Genoa when Sarah jabbed at a spot on the map, a town. We didn't recognise the name.

'Let's stop here,' she said.

Levanto. It nestled in a crook at the base of a series of mountains that rolled like an after-wash from the Alps down into the sea. There were olive groves, steeply terraced vineyards and churches clinging precariously to the hillside. We stood by the water in the early evening. Children played in the shallows while grandmothers kept watch from the shore. I was on the point of getting down on my knees; the words had been worked out, and the ring, fashioned from the lid of a beer bottle, was tucked in my pocket. Then, an intervention. On the beach a man died, quite quietly, without fuss, lying on his towel. We watched the crowd gather, the ambulance, the *Croce Rossa*. By the time it was over, the beach cleared, the moment had passed.

In 2002 my first novel, *Old Tom*, was published. I dedicated it to Sarah. *For Sarah. For Love.* It didn't set the world on fire, but it did attract a handful of positive reviews. The following year my agent, Peter Strange, suggested that I enter the National Short Story Prize. This was a new prize, inaugurated to inject life into what was thought to be a moribund art form. The prize money was significant, £15,000. Despite the money, I told Peter I didn't have anything appropriate.

'Don't be a prat,' he said. 'You're hot shit at the moment. You'll have a chance.'

Still, I didn't have anything. Peter persisted.

'Go through your drawers. You'll have something. Tidy it up. Wing it over to me. If you can't find something, bang something new out. It's only 5,000 words.'

I sat in the back bedroom and thought hard. I remembered. I did have something. 'How It Will End'. I had almost forgotten about it. It was still there, in the bottom drawer under some folders of household correspondence. I still hadn't told Sarah about it. It was the only thing I had kept from her. I looked at it. It was dreadful. I couldn't send it. Then Peter phoned.

'Got anything? Deadline's end of the month. Come on. I'm relying on you.'

I went back to the story. It took two weeks of hard work. I convinced myself that it wasn't about us, about me and Sarah. Even so, I didn't tell her anything. I reasoned that it would never see the light of day. Either Peter would tell me it was awful, or the judges would toss it aside without anything more than a cursory look. I sent it over to Peter two days before the deadline.

'It's fucking brilliant,' he said on the 'phone. 'Sensational. You're going to win this bastard, I can feel it.'

Weeks passed. I was like a criminal whose crime hasn't been discovered. Then, a letter. I had made the longlist of twelve, which would be cut down to a shortlist of five in due course. I had to go out to pick up some photographs that Sarah had taken the weekend before at Dunwich on the Suffolk coast. When I got back, Sarah was in the kitchen, the letter in her hand.

'This is brilliant news. Why didn't you tell me?'

I didn't say anything.

'I've put some champagne in the fridge. I thought we could have a little drink to celebrate.'

Her eyes were shining, so happy.

'I don't recognize the name of the story. 'How It Will End'. Have I seen it?'

I went out while she read it—I said I needed some cigarettes. In the story, as I imagined it that first night, I had seen our end in our beginning. I thought it was odd, even then, that I should see so much at the start; but then, is it so different from Beckett's image of birth astride a grave? Love, like life, only travels in one direction. The beginning is where the end starts. The end *is* in the beginning. On that score, at least, it was legitimate. When I first re-discovered it in the drawer, it was rough, quite general, and, at a push, I could probably deny that it was about us. But in the process of revision I added episodes, things that had actually happened. Blackwater. Levanto. Paris. It all went in.

I had always imagined the end coming because of something insignificant, something bizarre; something that would come out of nowhere, like that cloud formation that raced across the sky that night on Northey.

When I got back she was sitting in the kitchen, her head in her hands, the story on the table in front of her.

'How could you?'

'I'm sorry.'

'Is this it?' She picked the story up and then let it fall. It slid off the table and on to the floor. 'Is that what I am? Is that all I've ever been? Fucking material? For your precious career?'

'Hang on,' I said. 'I'm doing this for us.'

'Don't you fucking dare.'

James Salter, the American novelist and short-story writer, has a story. It is called 'Give'. In it, with his customary elegance, his coolness and concision, he describes the life of a young couple who devise a system to prevent the habitual annoyances of married life spiralling out of control. Salter calls it 'a way of getting the pebble out of the shoe'. It is the 'give' system. It works like this. If either partner has an unappealing habit, or tic, something small or insignificant that over time might develop in such a way as to irritate the other beyond proportion, the partner is allowed to ask for a 'give'. A give is a request to abandon.

It is a way of calling a truce, of stepping back from the brink before something insignificant becomes unmanageable.

Had I known of the 'give' system, I would have asked for one then, when I saw that look in Sarah's face. *Don't you fucking dare.*

'Give,' I would have said. 'Please, please. Give.'

She left. It wasn't entirely because of the story. That just served to widen some cracks that had always been there, beneath the surface, real cracks hidden by unreal love. It happened five years ago, nearly six. Last summer, she married someone else.

In *A Lover's Discourse*, Roland Barthes proposes that the act of falling in love follows on from being told stories about the act of falling in love. 'However particular,' he writes, 'amorous desire is discovered by induction.' We believe, in other words, what stories have taught us to believe, and our belief in love, as in most other things, is a construct of our culture. We write stories, but, at the same time, stories write us: they tell us what to do, what to think, what to feel. We fall in love; love falls in us. With that, we are back somewhere near the beginning. All stories are love stories. Stories love stories. Love loves love. Love stories love love stories.

Since Sarah left, I have published two further novels. I dedicated them both to her. *For S. Still.* I suppose I should stop, but I find that I don't want to. I find that I know how Norman Hart must have felt, that consuming blackness, as if there is no line between life and death. Still I hope that one day I will go to answer the door and she will be there on the step with a bag, that strand of hair slipping down from behind her ear.

'Give given,' she will say. 'Give given.'

I'm even writing a story about it. Right now. At the moment. In this instant. Unlike love, the story never ends. It never ends. It never ends. It never ends. It never ends. It never ends. It never ends. It never ends. It never ends. It never ends. ——

# No Angel

THE FIRST TIME I saw my father after he died, I was in the shower, hair plastered with conditioner, when the water stuttered and turned cold. He was at the sink in front of the misted-up mirror with the tap running, his back to me. It was two weeks after his funeral. His things were all where he'd left them.

'Them tiles would need re-grouting,' he said, and pointed his razor at the salmon-pink mould that was growing below the mirror.

I stared at him through the circle I'd wiped in the shower door. 'I didn't know you'd be able to do that,' I said.

'Oh yes,' he said, 'any decent tradesman would sort that out for you.' The twitch of a smile; thran as before.

He looked more or less the same. When he turned his face to scrape the razor along his jaw, I could see that the scar was healing well, where the surgeon had removed the growth from the side of his nose. His skin was more yellow maybe; more so at the nicotine-stained finger tips.

'Are they treating you well?' I asked him.

'So, so. The food's not great. Nothing seems to have much of a taste.'

'I suppose you empty the salt cellar over it still?'

'What harm's it going to do me now?'

I looked at him, at the thin white hair curling at the back of his neck from the steam in the bathroom; the earth under his fingernails.

'I'm getting cold,' I said.

'Don't worry,' he said, bending to splash water on his face, his knees creaking, 'I'm going now anyway,' and away he went.

The next time I saw him, I was on the train, on the way to Belfast sitting opposite a girl in a green bobble hat, when his face appeared in the window to my left. I looked back at the girl in her small round glasses, breaking off squares of chocolate with her teeth, at the umbilical iPod threading its way from her ear to her pocket. But outside, reflected in the glass, it was his face skimming over the fields. It was early December; there was a skin of snow on the hedges, green showing through; a slick of ice on the flooded grass. A bad time to spread slurry, he would have said. I'd never been on a train with him before.

'We used to ride to Knockarlet,' he said smiling his crooked smile, showing a bottom row of neglected teeth, 'me and your mother. Left the bikes at the station and took the train to the Port for the Big Sunday. It's years since I was on a train.' He spoke the way he had always spoken in his later years, like he was suppressing wind. Like the next sound that emitted from his mouth might be an involuntary one. People used to finish his sentences: he made them nervous of what was going to come out.

I loved that photo we had in the house, the pair of them strolling down the Prom arm in arm, her in her swing coat and curled hair, him in his wide lapels, a cigarette hanging off his right hand. They looked like film stars; the ghosts of their young selves. I used to pore over it as a teenager, wondering who they had been then, before me and then Robbie were born into their lives; before we wrenched love from them, and left again.

Above his head in the train window, were mirrored the orange letters of the information screen: 'Attention please. Passengers without a valid ticket please purchase one from the conductor.' He looked up, stuck out his elbow, nudged no-one in particular, winked in at me: 'Never let on you saw me!' he said.

Christmas week, I was invited out to dinner with Thomas's parents. Situation vacant: prospective daughter-in-law. I watched them process my details: a good lecturing job, attentive, soft-spoken, a bit long in the tooth for grandchildren, possibly, but these days you never know. They were far too middle class for religion to be an issue. The restaurant was over-heated; I'd gulped down too many nervous glasses of sauvignon blanc and had stepped outside for a breath of air. Daddy legged it out from a bus shelter on the far side of the road; dodged over between breaks in the headlights, a greasy brown paper bag in his hand.

'Are you going to marry thawn boy?' he said. Not so much as a 'Hullo'.

'You know his name, Daddy.'

'Are you going to marry him?'

'He hasn't asked me.'

He sighed through his nose, and his breath came out in two puffs of mist. 'I never knew you were that oul-fashioned,' he said. The smell of chip fat and vinegar.

'What's in the bag?' I said.

'You didn't answer me.'

'Neither did you.'

A couple came out the restaurant door; a blast of voices and heat, garlic and alcohol.

'He'll never set foot on my farm,' he said.

'He's a Maths teacher, Daddy. He doesn't want your farm.'

'He says that now,' he grunted. 'But they're all the same: hungry land grabbers every last one of them. He'll not get it. Not after what we went through to keep it.' He wrung the paper bag into a twist, fired it into a nearby bin.

'Not everybody's after your land, Daddy.'

'Have you forgotten what they did to your brother, Annie? The way they left him, lying on the road like a bag of rubbish the binmen had forgotten to lift? What it did to your mother, to see him like that?'

I gritted my teeth: 'It wasn't Thomas did that.'

'Him or his kind. I make no difference between them.' The spit flew out of his mouth. Then he turned on his heel and strode down the street, some loose change heavy in the outside pocket of his green fleece, banging against his thigh, altering the hang of him. It had never occurred to me that the dead could be bitter still, could still feel loss.

My brother Robbie wasn't the son my father had had in mind for himself. Daddy was a teetotaller all his life: the only drink we ever had in the house was a drop of poteen he kept for a sick cow. And my father was quiet, rarely raised his voice, except maybe to curse at a referee, or a traffic warden. Robbie, on the other hand, was loud, drank too much, lost all his money on poker machines, stole fags out of Daddy's coat pocket, took no interest in cattle rearing. He had a great sense of himself as unquashable, shot his mouth off when the rest of us knew how to stay dumb; had never learnt caution the way most people had in our uneasy mixed community. Some of the time I admired him for it; wished I could speak without looking to the left and right of me first. He wasn't involved in anything, people round here would have known that: if he had been, Daddy would have knocked it out of him himself. All he wanted was to join a rock band and 'get the hell out of this backwater'. The eighties were a nervous time, and things were worse after something big: Lough-gall, Enniskillen, Milltown, Ballygawley. Those were the times when people walked about careful, eyes to the ground. Robbie never eyed the ground. You'd think, then, he'd have seen it coming, what hit him in the face. A mallet, the coroner said, the type that was used to bash in fenceposts. They never found it.

Strange thing, though, he walked like Daddy: shoulders forward, great loping strides. Three years younger than me, and every step of his was one and a half of mine. I could never keep up with him. He was seventeen and built like a stick and mad about his guitar. He'd just failed his driving test and had called in the pub, where he shouldn't have been, and was walking home. They must have followed him out. It was December, dark by four and bone-cold. The coroner said he thought a car had hit him: after the beating, he said, when he had been left on the road. He couldn't be sure but there was evidence the body had been dragged. It was a neighbour that found him, picked him out in the car headlights. Daddy insisted on an open coffin, despite Robbie's eyebrow like a burst plum, his buckled nose, the rainbow of bruises that spanned his battered face. Despite Mum saying, 'Let people remember him the way he was.'

'No,' he'd insisted. 'Let everybody see what they did to him. Let everybody look and know what savages we're living amongst.'

They never got anybody for it, but ever since, there's

been neighbours of ours that couldn't look us in the eye. Mum lasted six months of barely speaking, food hardly passing her lips. She dropped like a stone one day in the kitchen; never spoke again. 'Your mother,' Daddy said to me, like he had to apologise for her leaving, '. . . her heart never mended.' Then it was just me and him, for nearly twenty-two years, until his lungs gave way, and the breath left him too.

In one of the bad times, around Hallowe'en, a month or two before Robbie was killed, I was home from University and Mum asked me to go in the front room and bring her in the sewing basket that she kept under the bed. I knelt down on the burgundy carpet, lifted the valance sheet, and there was the shotgun, quiet as you like. Daddy had always kept one: he and Uncle Joe went shooting for pheasant every Boxing Day. And if there was a wedding in the townland, he'd take it out, shoot a cartridge or two in the air to send the bride off. But the rest of the time, he kept it locked up in the built-in wardrobe. He was normally very careful about it. I carried the basket back in to the kitchen.

'Why's the gun under your bed?'

'Thread that for me, will you?' she said. She sat with Daddy's good trousers on her lap, pressing the unravelled hem between her finger and thumb. I held the needle up to the light, laced the grey thread through. 'Two or three times,' she said, 'a car has driven into the yard at night. No lights: we hear the wheels on the gravel.' She took the needle from me, wound a knot into the end of the thread. 'Your father says if any of them tries to get in, he'll shoot first, ask questions later.'

'Why would anybody . . .?'

'There's people, Annie, that needs no excuse. We're

the wrong sort for them, that's all; in the wrong place. They'd like to see the back of us.' And she pushed the needle into the hem and started to sew.

I was glad to get back to Belfast. The threat in the city never felt personal. A bomb scare on University Road and everybody piled back into bed: lectures cancelled for the morning. The night the explosion went off at the Lisburn Road police station, the whole of our rented house shook. Eight girls on the landing in their pyjamas and then down to the kitchen to stand bare-footed on the cracked, snail-slimed lino, warming our hands around cups of tea, listening for the sirens: second-hand drama. Not like a dark car in your own yard at night; not like a shotgun under the bed.

The next time I saw my father after he died, it was night and I was driving over the bog road near Castlenagree with the windscreen wipers doing battle against the rain, and Bob Dylan on the radio, 'Like a Rolling Stone'. I'd turned the music up full and was giving it welly: 'How does it feel . . .?'

'What's that oul' shite you're listening to?' he said, and near put me off the road. A twitter of a laugh: 'That would deave you,' and his arm reached out, and turned down the dial. There was a green light off the dashboard; my fists tight on the steering wheel. 'What happened your hand?' he said. A small black crescent of soot ingrained above my knuckles.

'You know rightly what happened it,' I told him, 'putting the life out of me in the coal house last night. I hit it against the shovel.' He was silent. The sound of his skin-roughened finger and thumb, rubbing together. 'Knocking the door against the back of my heels,' I said. 'You know I don't like the dark.'

'It was maybe the wind.'

'There wasn't a breath. You needn't deny it. I smelt Benson & Hedges.'

'I've given up the smokes,' he said. 'They were a shocking price, getting.'

'Your timing's not great.'

The rain was coming down harder, troughing water along the sides of the road. I could smell the damp wool of his jacket, drying in the fan, and something underneath it, something familiar, coal tar soap.

'Does this seat not go back?' he said, grappling for the lever at the side. 'That Thomas boy must be a right short-arse. My knees is killing me.' I was silent, not rising to the bait, and then, 'Do you remember,' he said, 'the night you swallowed the two-p bit?'

I did. I was five, six maybe. I can still feel the chink of metal against my teeth; taste the copper, feel the wrong shape of it slide down my throat. I don't know what upset me more: the swallowing of it, or the disappointment at the loss of the money. I hadn't made the connection between food and waste: was stunned when Mum said I wasn't to flush the toilet till she was sure it had passed. And every morning, the same line from him and Robbie . . .

'Any change?' he said in the seat beside me, his whole body shaking.

That was the night he told me the story of Ali Baba and the Forty Thieves. And when he said the part about the robbers hiding in the urns, I didn't know the word, so he said, 'You know, urns, big containers, like tea chests. That's what we'll call them. The thirty-nine robbers hid in the tea chests and the captain went into the house.' It was nearly worth swallowing the coin for: the candy-striped sheets in their big bed, and the light coming in under the crack in the door and 'Ali Baba' in his turban and the blind cobbler and the clever servant-girl and the robbers in the tea chests. And the burst-open brother they had to sew back together again.

'You know, Annie. I would never scare you like that. That wasn't me at the coal house door.'

I kept my eyes on the road as we rounded a bend. Then I said, 'Daddy, do you ever see . . .?' but when I turned my head, the seat beside me was empty.

He needn't have bothered with the jibes about Thomas: we didn't last. I think it was Thomas's confidence I fell for: his belief in my ability to love him back; his faith in the world's acceptance of us both. He never questioned his right to be anywhere. He was entirely without arrogance but he stood and talked and put one foot after the other with absolute unshakeable conviction. I think, maybe, if I'm honest, he reminded me of Robbie. It was never going to work. I wouldn't have been able to keep up the suitable daughter-in-law show for a whole lifetime.

Daddy made occasional appearances after that. One Tuesday afternoon after the spring term had started, I looked out from a lecture hall of second-year students who cared little for Molière or the Commedia dell'Arte, and I saw him, intent, climbing a grass bank, heading towards the University Arboretum with a hazel stick in his hand, his corduroy trousers bagging at the knees. I got the impression he was following someone.

Then one night in May at the Opera House, a staff outing to *The Bartered Bride* and me bored witless, I tore my eyes away from Marenka in her embroidered apron and glanced up at the boxes and there he was: good grey suit, opera glasses in his hand. He who had never set foot in a theatre in his life.

'What are you doing here?' I mouthed up at him.

'Keeping an eye on him,' he said and he stuck out his elbow and nudged the man beside him: Robbie, in an over-sized bow tie, with his face back the way it used to be. 'I told you it wasn't me at the coal house door.'

Robbie was scanning the audience. 'There she is,' he said, and pointed to a small woman, three rows ahead in a turquoise dress with winged shoulder pads. The woman turned and looked up and waved: Mum out in her finery. Neither she nor Robbie looked at me.

'You found them,' I said.

'I did,' Daddy said.

'They look well.' He nodded and smiled. 'Will you leave me alone now?' I asked him.

He looked down at his hands. 'I was right about thawn Thomas boy,' he said. 'He wasn't your match.'

'I won't be told who to love by you,' I said.

'I know.'

I looked around at the packed auditorium, at Mum's shining eyes, back up at him and Robbie. 'I'll see you, then,' I said.

I could see his mouth move. 'You know where we are,' he said, and then the song ended, and the audience rose up in applause and blocked my view with their bellowing elbows and the backs of their nodding heads.

# Slut's Hair

T HE TOOTH HAD been bothering her all day, and that was why she told Rob about it. She hadn't wanted to, and she knew it was a mistake telling him anything, but then everything she did these days was a mistake, and she couldn't go on forever, day and night, being careful what she said and, at the same time, not seeming to keep things from him, because that made him angrier than anything else. A wife shouldn't have secrets from her husband, he would say. If there was one thing he hated, it was secrets. He had asked her what was wrong when they were sitting down to eat, though she didn't know why, because she hadn't said a word about it. If she had, he would only have told her to stop complaining. He didn't like people who complained all the time, instead of just getting on with it. So, even though the tooth was all inflamed and throbbing by the time he got in, she'd been careful not to let on that she was hurting—and she didn't see how he could have known, because she'd kept the pain to herself, and just got on with making his dinner. But then, he was like that sometimes. It was as if he could read her mind.

'So,' he had said, out of the blue, as she brought him his Tennent's. 'What's wrong with Janice now?' She had made spaghetti again, because pasta was cheap, even though he didn't like to have the same thing too often. She reckoned if she used different sauces, like tomato one night, then maybe bacon and mushroom a couple of nights later, it wouldn't seem like too much of the same. He liked pasta, so it wasn't as bad as if it was rice, or mash. 'Are you sickening for something?' he said.

Janice forced a smile and poured the lager. He didn't like a big head on his beer, so she had to concentrate on that. Everything had to be just so. 'I'm fine,' she said, keeping her voice quiet, so it didn't sound like she was whining. Rob hated it when she whined.

'Well, you're obviously not,' he said. 'You're going round with a face like a dog's arse, so you're not fine, are you?'

He gave her a bright, conclusive smile, then carried on eating. It wasn't fair. She looked after her teeth; he never did. But then, he never had any problems with his health. Especially not with his teeth. He hadn't been to the dentist's in years, he would say. Not since school, in fact.

They were all thieves, dentists. Sometimes, when he was at a barbecue or a party, he would prise the top off a beer-bottle with his front teeth and spit it out with a big grin. Then he would tip the bottle up and down it in one, the froth gurgling over the rim and running down his chin. 'I've just got a bit of a toothache,' she said. 'It'll soon pass.'

Rob picked up his fork and twirled the pasta round on it. Bits of mushroom and grated cheese spun out across the table, but he didn't notice. He really did like pasta and, usually, it put him in a good mood for the rest of the evening if they had spaghetti Bolognese, or that nice penne and seafood recipe she'd got out of the paper. He'd worked in an Italian restaurant one time, and he could tell you all the names of the different pasta shapes. Vermicelli. Fusilli. Linguine. Bucatini. Spaccatelli. He'd only been a kitchen porter, but he knew them all. 'It bloody well better,' he said, when he'd finally collected a good forkful. 'You can't go wandering around with a face like that.' He put the fork in his mouth and bit off the loose ends of spaghetti, then he took a sip of his beer. 'It's depressing,' he said.

Janice looked at her plate. She didn't feel like eating now, the pain was that bad, but she knew she would have to. He couldn't stand waste. 'I'll be fine,' she said, hoping to have done with it. Rob didn't say anything then, so she tried a mouthful of spaghetti. The sauce was hot and sharp in her mouth, but she swallowed it down anyway. 'Oh, for Christ's sake!' he said, letting his cutlery fall to the table. Janice put hers down too and waited. The thing to do, when he was angry, was to stop everything and let him say what he needed to say. He sat quietly for a moment, considering, then he took a sip of his lager and sat back. 'What's wrong with it anyway?'

'It's just a bit tender,' she said.

'Well, is it rotten?'

'I don't think so—'

'There must be something wrong with it,' he said. He stood up and walked round the table to where she was sitting. 'Let's have a look.' He took her by the chin and pushed her head back.

'Open wide,' he said.

She opened her mouth. She realised, as she did, that she had bad breath and she didn't want him to smell it. 'I don't think—'

'I can't see when your gums are flapping,' he said. He brought his face close to hers, so she could smell the beer. It was like when they had sex, on Saturday nights, that beer smell in her nose and mouth, him moving her about like a doll. 'Which one is it?' he said, twisting her head around to get a better light.

'It's—'

'Ah!' He released her suddenly and stepped back. 'Well,' he said. 'You've really let that go. Is this the first you've noticed?'

Janice didn't say anything. There was nothing to say. She'd known the tooth was bad, but she also knew that she couldn't go to a dentist. They were all private now, and even when they weren't, they still cost money. These days, she didn't have enough for the housekeeping, never mind the dentist. So it was pointless talking about it and, in the meantime, the food would be getting cold. He'd probably blame her for that, too.

'Well,' Rob said. 'You'll have to get it seen to.'

She stared at her spaghetti. 'I'm sure it will pass,' she said. 'Anyway, it's too expensive.'

That shut him up for a minute. He hated it when she talked about money. He hated it, that she was always so negative, always going on about what they couldn't afford. But then, even he knew how little they had, now that she wasn't working any more, and him being only casual. It had been all right when she was still at the hospital, but he'd made her give that up, because the early start time didn't work with his schedule. She'd liked that job, too. Playing with the kids when they first came in, then making sure the grown-ups were all right when the little ones went into theatre. Mostly, the parents didn't know how badly it would affect them, when little Angela or Tommy went under, there one moment, gone the next. It was a shock, seeing that happen—and then they had to go out and wait on the ward till some complete stranger was finished working on their child with swabs and scalpels. Some of them got pretty upset and it was Janice's role to be with them then and provide reassurance. That was a big responsibility—and she'd hated Rob when he'd told her that she had to give it up. But then, he couldn't have understood what it was like, because he'd never had a job like that, where you were dealing with people on a regular basis.

Rob was back in his chair now, drinking his beer. Janice could see that he was thinking, which wasn't a good sign. She wound some spaghetti round her fork. Maybe, if she just went on as normal, he would let it go.

'You're right,' he said, after a moment. 'It's too expensive.' He finished the beer, then set the glass on the table and gave her a pointed look. Janice got up immediately and went to the fridge for another tin. She opened it carefully, and put it down where he could reach it easily. She only had to pour the first one. After that, he poured his own. She sat down and started on another forkful of spaghetti.

'Forget that,' he said, his voice suddenly hard. Not loud, not yet, though that would come. He thought for a moment, then he got up and walked through to the hall. She could hear him rummaging around in the cupboard by the front door and she wondered what he was doing. He wasn't gone long though and when he came back he was carrying his toolbox. He looked at her.

'I'll fix it,' he said.

She didn't understand at first. 'Fix what?' she said. Then she did understand and before she could stop herself, she shook her head. 'No,' she said—and she knew immediately that she had made a mistake. Rob didn't say anything, though; he just opened the toolbox and took out a pair of fine pliers, the kind electricians use.

'See,' he said. 'I've got everything the dentist has, in

my toolbox. It might not be as shiny, but with all that money he's raking in, he can afford to have shiny new pliers.' He looked her in the eye. 'But that's all it takes, when it comes down to it. A pair of pliers and a firm hand.'

Janice shook her head, but she didn't say anything. If she tried to disagree, he definitely wouldn't let it go. Not unless she had a practical reason why he couldn't do it. He was rummaging through the toolbox now, checking to see what else might come in useful. 'But, Rob,' she said, after a moment. She always felt strange when she said his name. It was like repeating a lie. 'It's not safe. It's not—sterile—'

'No problemo,' he said. 'All we need is boiling water. Like in the Westerns.'

She thought about this for a moment—and for that one moment she thought it might be a joke after all. But when he went through to the kitchen and put the kettle on, she knew he was serious. 'Please, Rob,' she said. 'Your food's getting cold.'

He didn't answer. She could hear him clattering about in the kitchen, getting something out of the press, and then the kettle boiled and he came back with a glass and a bottle of whisky that he'd won in a raffle at work. He didn't like whisky that much, so he'd hardly touched it. He put the bottle on the table, then set the glass next to it. 'Drink this,' he said.

'I'm all right,' she said. 'It's not hurting so much now.' She could hear the desperation in her voice, which meant that he could hear it too. That would only make him more determined to finish what he had started.

He ignored her. 'Anaesthetic,' he said. 'That's how they do it in the films. When they're cutting a bullet out, or something.' He took his pliers and went back to the kitchen and, for one brief instant, it crossed her mind that she could run. If she was fast, she could get out the door and be halfway downstairs before he noticed. But she didn't move. He came back with the newly sterilised pliers. 'All set,' he said. He looked at the empty glass. 'You'd better drink some of that. It'll make things a lot easier.' He set the pliers down carefully on the table, so the points didn't touch anything. 'Don't be a baby,' he said, pouring her a big glassful of the whisky. 'It'll be over before you know it.' He handed her the glass. 'Drink.'

She took the glass and raised it to her lips. The whisky smelled sweet and dark, like damp wood. She swallowed down as much as she could in one, then she swallowed again to stop from being sick. Rob stood over her until the glass was empty, then he poured another and watched till she drank that.

Then, when it was all gone, he went to work.

Afterwards, she sat in front of the TV for a long time with a towel pressed to her face while Rob got ready to go out. He hadn't said anything about it when he got home, but as soon as he'd finished pulling the tooth and got himself cleaned up, he'd announced that he had to go and see Dougie down the West End. 'I'll not be long, though,' he said. He always said that—and sometimes it was true. Sometimes he would only be gone an hour. Other times he would stay out until the early morning. He liked to keep her on her toes.

He had hurt her badly this time. The tooth wouldn't come out at first, and he'd had to force it, holding her in the chair with one hand while he yanked at her jaw with the other, muttering and cursing all the time, and shouting at her to keep still so he could get a grip. At one point, the pliers had slipped, and she'd been scared that he would break one of her good teeth, but he'd kept going till it finally came loose. It took a long time, though. By the end, there was blood everywhere, on him and on her face and T-shirt, and Janice had felt sick again, from the pain and the whisky.

There was nothing on the TV. She wasn't really watching anyway, but after a while it started to depress her, so she turned it off and walked over to the window. The street below was invisible now, except for the silvery glow coming up from the shop fronts and she could see, across the roofs of the houses opposite, the twinkle and glitter of the city winding up to the Hilltown. Most of the time, it seemed grey and damp, but when it was just lights in the dark like this, it could be really beautiful. When you couldn't see the people or the cars, it was almost peaceful, almost the life she had wanted when she had first known Rob. He had been different then, and she had thought they both wanted the same things: the quiet at night, evenings at home together, relaxing music and a nice meal that she had spent hours preparing.

She remembered how he'd taken her out one Sunday afternoon when he still had the car, and they'd gone across to Fife, all the way down past St Andrews to this beach he knew near Kingsbarns. He had gone there when he was just a kid, he said, and he'd been happy in that place, which was why he wanted to share it with her. It wasn't much, and he'd been shy about it as they walked across the beach, looking out over the water. It was a cold, clear winter's afternoon, just before Christmas. There were no other people, so it was quiet too, except for the slow power of the sea, the white surge of it almost reaching their feet before streaming back in thin, glistening layers across the sand. They had walked for an hour or more, picking their way back and forth through the rock pools and the deeper soakaways that streamed down off the fields and, at the end, when she looked up, it was still day, but the moon was there, white and flaky above the water, like a chalk mark. She had been so happy that afternoon. She had loved that beach and she had loved Rob for taking her there—and it surprised her now, remembering, that it had only been three years ago.

Three years. That was all the time it had taken for him to become somebody she didn't know, and make her into somebody she didn't recognise in the mirror, somebody who had given up her job because he told her to, somebody who could sit in a chair at the kitchen table and let him prise her teeth out with electrician's pliers. Now, she was sick and in pain, and all she wanted to do was get away from him, but she knew she couldn't. She was too scared. He'd told her often enough, when he'd been drinking, that he couldn't live without her, how, if she ever left him, he didn't know what he would do. He always said that, after he'd done something bad. Tonight, probably, he'd come home with a bar of chocolate or a bottle of Babycham, and he'd sit her down at the kitchen table and tell her how sorry he was and how much he really loved her. He would ask her to forgive him, and she would, because she was scared of what would happen to her if she didn't. Then, if he wasn't too drunk, they would go to bed and he would do that thing he'd read about in *Forum*.

It was when she went back into the kitchen to get some more Anadin, that she heard the noise. It was just a rustle and, at first, she couldn't tell exactly where it was coming from. She stood at the open cupboard, counting out the pills—there were only eight of them, not enough for an overdose—and she heard the rustling noise in the corner, between the fridge and the press, or maybe in among the pipes at the back, where the dust gathered.

Rob was always complaining to her about the kitchen, how she didn't clean behind things properly and that was like an open invitation for vermin to settle down and build nests and have little itty bitty children of their own. He would do that last part in his Gary Oldman in *The Fifth Element* voice: he loved that film and he pretty well knew the script off by heart. Anyone else wanna negotiate? he would say, in his Bruce Willis voice and Dougie and the others would think he was so funny, only it wasn't funny at all, because there was always a streak of nastiness running through it. At home, when he did those voices, she always knew he was gearing up for something. Bingo! he'd say, doing Gary Oldman as the bent cop in *Leon*, whenever he caught her out, or found something she'd messed up. He'd done it so often, she got scared whenever Gary Oldman was on the telly. It didn't matter what film he was in. She got so scared, she could feel it in her chest and throat, like a scream she couldn't get out.

She took two of the Anadin, and washed them down with some water. Rob had left the whisky on the kitchen table and she thought about drinking more of it. Maybe with the pills it would make her sick enough so she'd have to go to the hospital, but she knew that was no good either. That would just be showing Rob up, and she would have to pay for it, sooner or later. She stood a moment, trying to get her head straight. She didn't feel drunk at all, just woozy and battered. If she went to bed and pretended to be asleep, maybe he wouldn't bother her when he got back. Maybe he would be too drunk for sex and he'd just get in beside her and pass out. Best would be if he got a carry-out and went back to Dougie's, of course, but there wasn't much hope of that. Not unless Dougie had the money to sub him, which was unlikely. Her mind was going round in circles now and she knew she shouldn't have taken more pills, not on top of all that whisky. She thought about having a shower, but her mind rebelled at that—she wanted to have blood on her when he came in, so he wouldn't forget what he had done. She wanted to look a mess, so he wouldn't want to have sex, though she didn't suppose he'd care what she looked like, if he came back steaming. He probably wouldn't even notice.

The noise came again and this time she pinpointed it exactly. It was in the far corner, by the tumble-dryer her mum had given them—and now that she looked, she could see something, though she couldn't make out what it was. Her vision was blurry, and what she could see was something vague and unfinished, like a scribble in blue ink among the wet shadows—something impossible, she thought, though it was definitely there. A misshapen clutch of blue fur, half-formed and not quite solid, like that stuff you find under the bed in some old person's house, where nobody's done any cleaning for years. That was what it looked like, for a moment; but then it moved, and that sound came again, first a rustle, then a scratching sound, like an animal trying to burrow through damp plaster. Which was exactly what it was, she saw, as she moved closer and peered into the powdery, Persil-scented nook of dirty-white linoleum between the tumble-dryer and the wall: an animal, though what kind of animal she couldn't say, because her eyes were so blurry and the shadows made it difficult to see.

At first, she thought it looked like a tiny, malnourished cat, only it was blue and too small even for a kitten; then, as her eyes adjusted, she saw that it was a fox, or something like a fox, with that keen, clever face a fox has in children's books. The quick brown fox jumps over the lazy dog. Only that was impossible, because foxes weren't blue and, anyway, how would a fox get into her kitchen, high up on the third floor of a tenement block in the middle of Dundee? And how could a fox be so small? Because now that she looked closely, she could see that it was small, far too small for a fox or a kitten or even a rat. It was tiny—which meant that it had to be something else, something possible. Maybe a mouse that had escaped from some kid's house and crawled up here to be safe. You could get pet mice in all different colours now: white, black, yellow and probably, for all she knew, they had blue ones too. She bent closer and stared at the thing, as it pressed against the wall, scratching desperately at the damp plaster—and now that her eyes were getting clearer, she could see that it really was a mouse. A small, long-haired, powder-blue mouse with tiny feet and a sharp, clever face, gazing up at her from the shadows. She was surprised to realise that she wasn't afraid, but the animal was. It was terrified, in fact, and desperate to get out, scared and lost and far from its own kind, its wet, black eyes gazing up at her, so shiny and wet and hopeless that she felt a sudden, desperate need to gather it up and spirit it away before Rob got home. To save it, in other words—because Rob would kill it, if he found it there. It wouldn't matter that it was blue and somebody's pet, he would kill it anyway, because he hated vermin. He would kill it without a second thought and Janice knew that she couldn't let that happen. She had to pick the thing up and get it out of there, maybe let it loose on the stairs and see if it found its own way home or, better yet, carry it out to the little drying green behind the tenements and set it down in the grass, so it could scuttle off into the dark.

She needed to save it—she didn't know why but she had to—and, really, it wasn't that big a deal. All she had to do was be confident, like her granddad had told her to be, when she was little and still living at home. Back then, the neighbourhood kids would always be coming by to tell him about a hurt thrush or a starling they had found in the woods, or out on the old farm road and, when they did, he would immediately put down what he was doing and follow them out to where the bird was, a big, calm man in his shirtsleeves, surrounded by hushed, excited boys. Then, half an hour later, he would come back, the bird still and watchful in his hand, attentive to all that was happening, but not really scared, because it sensed the gentleness in him. He'd explained to her, once, how that was all it took, when you were dealing with animals and birds. If you were calm, they were calm. If you were scared, they would be scared. All she had to do was be confident.

Only, she had no idea how to catch a living animal, and even after she'd told herself that it was just a tiny thing, alone and defenceless and probably more terrified than she was, it still frightened her. Nevertheless, she forced herself to hunker down and make a cradle of her hands, willing the mouse to be still just long enough for her to scoop it up out of this dim, soap-scented corner and carry it away. She didn't know what time it was, but she knew that Rob might come back at any minute. So she had to be quick, and she had to be decisive. Decisive and confident and, most of all, calm.

She got down on one knee. The mouse had stopped moving and turned slightly and, though it wasn't looking at her any more, it knew she was there. It didn't panic, though, and it didn't try to run away as, inch by inch, she closed in. Then, suddenly, her hand darted out, of its own volition—one hand, not two, as she had originally intended—and she had the mouse in her half-closed fist, a little sack of hair and bones, not struggling, not moving at all, in fact, and utterly silent. For a moment, every-thing was still. She lifted her hand slightly to peer at the mouse—and it seemed at first that she had missed alto-gether and scooped up nothing but dust and air. Then, as she brought her half-closed fist closer, she saw its face. She couldn't tell what it was thinking, but it didn't look scared any more, it just seemed to be listening for something, far off in the distance.

It had ears that were too large for its head and its mouth looked tiny and clenched, as if someone had stitched it shut with fine black thread. Before, she had thought it would be plump and round and warm in her fist; now that she had it, she could feel how cold and insubstantial it was. That surprised her more than anything. It was nothing, really, the merest wisp of a thing that she couldn't help thinking would vanish altogether, if she tightened her grip any further—and even before she turned to go into the other room, even before she heard Rob's key in the front door, she could feel it shrinking, so that, for one brief moment, she thought she was crushing it, even though her hand was so careful, so soft. That was what she had been afraid of, when she first thought to pick it up: she hadn't been scared for herself, she had been afraid she would hurt the mouse in some way, without meaning to. She was afraid it would die, and it would be her fault. Yet now, as it sat snug in her hand, safe and hidden and warm, it was melting away, dwindling between her fingers to the merest clutch of hair and dust—and she knew that she'd have to get it out of the flat before it disappeared altogether.

She had only gone a couple of steps when she heard the key. First the key, then the door swinging open with that slight creak it had, and then—moment by moment, like some slow motion soundtrack of everyday life—the sound of Rob taking off his coat and coming through, his face distant and slightly bleared from the drink. At first, he didn't even see her, standing there in the doorframe between the living room and the kitchen, and she knew he'd had a good skinful, though it hardly seemed any time at all since he'd left. Then he made her out and stood a long moment, like someone peering through fog, and it reminded her of the parents in the waiting room, after their children had gone in to surgery, how they looked at her from so far away, unhappy and surprised, as if they couldn't quite remember who she was.

She had only gone a couple of steps and, all the time, as she stood facing her husband, trying to decide how drunk he might be, she could feel the last trace of the mouse wasting away — until, finally, in this state of suspended animation, she began to realise that she hadn't caught the mouse at all. She had missed it altogether and come up with nothing more than a fistful of dust and — what was that stuff you found in dark corners where nobody had cleaned? What was it called?

Slut's hair. Yes; that was it. That was what her mother had always called it — slut's hair — and Janice remembered how much she had liked the sound of those words when she was little, before she knew what a slut was. Rob had called her that, once, when she'd let Dougie kiss her under the mistletoe — a fleeting brush of his lips on her cheek, not really a kiss at all — that first Christmas after they'd got married. Slut. He'd said it like he was happy, like he'd known it all along. 'You're just a little slut,' he'd said, and when she tried to laugh it off, he'd grabbed her by the throat and pushed her against the wall. 'What kind of idiot do you think I am?' he'd said, and he'd held her there till the tears came.

Now, he was staring at her, as if he was surprised not

to be coming home to an empty house, and she could see that he was even drunker than she'd thought. At the same time, the thought came to her that, if she hadn't caught it before, the mouse had to be somewhere behind her still—out of harm's way, at least for the moment—and she listened, hoping she wouldn't hear anything, praying that the animal had sensed Rob coming in and had scuttled away to some dark place where he would never find it. Because she needed that mouse to be safe. It was her secret, and she had to keep it from harm. Nothing is more precious than a secret, her granddad had told her once, when she was little—and she had treasured that idea all through her school years, because there had been nothing else to treasure. All her life, she had made up secrets, inventing them out of thin air and keeping them, religiously—and now she had one again. It was nothing but a mouse, she knew that, a tiny blue mouse with a stitched shut mouth and oversize ears, but it had come to her and nobody else, and Rob could never be allowed anywhere near it. Not now, not ever.

She felt woozy again, suddenly, and her jaw was throbbing. It must have been like that all the time, she realised, but she hadn't felt it until now. She looked at Rob. She had to make out that she was pleased to see him, she had to make him think she'd waited up for him all this time, so she could make him a coffee, or fetch him another drink, the moment he came in the door. Most of all, she had to pretend she didn't know he was drunk, because that would mean she was judging him, and he hated to be judged more than anything. She set her mouth in what she hoped was a smile. 'I was just going to put the kettle on,' she said, and she knew she was explaining herself already, which was bound to arouse his suspicions, because going to the kitchen wasn't something that needed explaining, even to him.

He wasn't suspicious, though, and she knew, with a bright surge of relief, that he wouldn't find the mouse. Not tonight, anyway. He was too drunk, and there was something else going on, a dark, bemused tangle of thoughts and emotions behind his eyes that she immediately recognised as something like regret. That was what he always did, after he'd hurt her badly.

He would get drunk and then he'd be guilty. Sometimes he would say he was sorry and he would make promises for the future, sometimes he would just come and stand in front of her, waiting for a sign that they could put it all behind them. For as long as it lasted, that feeling would be genuine—and she hated him for it. 'Do you want coffee?' she said.

Rob nodded, but he didn't say anything. He was still thinking, still rehearsing the pretty little speech he would make when he was ready. Janice waited a moment, then she went back to the kitchen to boil the kettle, taking care not to look in the direction of the tumble dryer until she heard the television come on. Then, when she was completely sure she wouldn't be seen, she went over to the exact spot where she had knelt before, to make sure there was nothing that Rob might see, other than some tiny scratches in the plaster and a few scattered wisps of slut's hair, strangely lifelike and blue against the dirty-white linoleum.

HILARY MANTEL

# Comma

I CAN SEE MARY Joplin now, in the bushes crouching with her knees apart, her cotton frock stretched across her thighs. In the hottest summer (and this was it) Mary had a sniffle, and she would rub the tip of her upturned nose, meditatively, with the back of her hand, and inspect the glistening snail-trail that was left. We squatted, both of us, up to our ears in tickly grass: grass which, as midsummer passed, turned from tickly to scratchy and etched white lines, like the art of a primitive tribe, across our bare legs. Sometimes we would rise together, as if pulled up by invisible strings. Parting the rough grass in swathes, we would push a little closer to where we knew we were going, and where we knew we should not go. Then, as if by some predetermined signal, we would flounce down again, so we would be half-invisible if God looked over the fields.

Buried in the grass we talked: myself monosyllabic, guarded, eight years old, wearing too-small shorts of black-and-white check, that had fitted me last year: Mary with her scrawny arms, her knee-caps like saucers of bone, her bruised legs, her snigger and her cackle and her snort. Some unknown hand, her own perhaps, had placed on her rat-tails a twisted white ribbon; by afternoon it had skewed itself around to the side, so that her head looked like a badly tied parcel. Mary Joplin put questions to me: 'Are you rich?'

I was startled. 'I don't think so. We're about middle. Are you rich?'

She pondered. She smiled at me as if we were comrades now. 'We're about middle too.'

Poverty meant upturned blue eyes and a begging bowl. A charity child. You'd have coloured patches sewn on your clothes. In a fairytale picture book you live in the forest under the dripping gables, your roof is thatch. You have a basket with a patchwork cover with which you venture out to your grandma. Your house is made of cake.

When I went to my grandma's it was empty-handed, and I was sent just to be company for her. I didn't know what this meant. Sometimes I stared at the wall till she let me go home again. Sometimes she let me pod peas. Sometimes she made me hold her wool while she wound it. She snapped at me to call me to attention if let my wrists droop. When I said I was weary, she said I didn't know the meaning of the word. She'd show me weary, she said. She carried on muttering: weary, I'll show her who's weary, I'll weary her with a good slap.

When my wrists drooped and my attention faltered it was because I was thinking of Mary Joplin. I knew not to mention her name and the pressure of not mentioning her made her, in my imagination, beaten thin and flat, attenuated, starved away, a shadow of herself, so I was no longer sure whether she existed when I was not with her. But then next day in the morning's first dazzle, when I stood on our doorstep, I would see Mary leaning against the house opposite, smirking, scratching herself under her frock, and she would stick her tongue out at me until it was stretched to the root.

If my mother looked out she would see her too; or maybe not.

On those afternoons, buzzing, sleepy, our wandering had a veiled purpose and we drew closer and closer to the Hathaways' house. I did not call it that then, and until that summer I hadn't known it existed; it seemed it had materialised during my middle childhood, as our boundaries pushed out, as we strayed further from the village's core. Mary had found it before I did. It stood on its own, no other house built on to it, and we knew without debate that it was the house of the rich; stone-built, with one lofty round tower, it stood in its gardens bounded by a wall, but not too high a wall for us to climb: to drop softly, between the bushes on the other side. From there we saw that in the beds of this garden the roses were already scorched into heavy brown blebs on the stalk. The lawns were parched. Long windows glinted, and around the house, on the side from which we approached, there ran a veranda or loggia or terrace; I did not have a word for it, and no use asking Mary.

She said cheerily, as we wandered cross-country, 'Me dad says, you're bloody daft, Mary, do you know that? He says, when they turned you out, love, they broke the bloody mould. He says, Mary, you don't know arseholes from Tuesday.'

On that first day at the Hathaway house, sheltered in the depth of the bushes, we waited for the rich to come out of the glinting windows that were also doors; we waited to see what actions they would perform. Mary Joplin whispered to me, 'Your mam dun't know where you are.'

'Well, your mam neither.'

As the afternoon wore on, Mary made herself a hollow or nest. She settled comfortably under a bush. 'If I'd known it was this boring,' I said, 'I'd have brought my library book.'

Mary twiddled grass stalks, sometimes hummed. 'My dad says, buck yourself up, Mary, or you'll have to go to reform school.'

'What's that?'

'It's where they smack you every day.'

'What've you done?'

'Nothing, they just do it.'

I shrugged. It sounded only too likely. 'Do they smack you on weekend or only school days?'

I felt sleepy. I hardly cared about the answer. 'You stand in a queue,' Mary said. 'When it's your turn . . .' Mary had a little stick which she was digging into the ground, grinding it round and round into the soil. 'When it's your turn, Kitty, they have a big club and they beat the holy living daylights out of you. They knock you on the head till your brains squirt out.'

Our conversation dried up: lack of interest on my part. In time my legs, folded under me, began to ache and cramp. I shifted irritably, nodded towards the house. 'How long do we have to wait?'

Mary hummed. Dug with her stick.

'Put your legs together, Mary,' I said. 'It's rude to sit like that.'

'Listen,' she said, 'I've been up here when a kid like you is in bed. I've seen what they've got in that house.'

I was awake now. 'What have they?'

'Something you couldn't put a name to,' Mary Joplin said.

'What sort of a thing?'

'Wrapped in a blanket.'

'Is it an animal?'

Mary jeered. 'An animal, she says. An animal, what's wrapped in a blanket?'

'You could wrap a dog in a blanket. If it were poorly.'

I felt the truth of this; I wanted to insist; my face grew hot. 'It's not a dog, no, no, no.' Mary's voice dawdled, keeping her secret from me. 'For it's got arms.'

'Then it's human.'

'But it's not a human shape.'

I felt desperate. 'What shape is it?'

Mary thought. 'A comma,' she said slowly. 'A comma, you know, what you see in a book?'

After this she would not be drawn. 'You'll just have to wait,' she said, 'if you want to see it, and if you truly do you'll wait, and if you truly don't you can bugger off and you can miss it, and I can see it all to myself.'

After a while I said, 'I can't stop here all night waiting for a comma. I've missed my tea.'

'They'll be none bothered,' Mary said.

She was right. I crept back late and nothing was said. It was a summer that, by the end of July, had bleached adults of their purpose. When my mother saw me her eyes glazed over, as if I represented extra effort. You spilled blackcurrant juice on yourself and you kept the sticky patches. Feet grimy and face stained you lived in underbrush and long grass, and each day a sun like a child's painted sun burned in a sky made white with heat. Laundry hung like flags of surrender from washing lines. The light stretched far into the evening, ending in a fall of dew and a bare dusk. When you were called in at last you sat under the electric light and pulled off your sunburnt skin in frills and strips. There was a dull roasting sensation deep inside your limbs, but no sensation as you peeled yourself like a vegetable.

You were sent to bed when you were sleepy, but as the heat of bed-clothes fretted your skin you woke again. You lay awake, wheeling fingernails over your insect bites. There was something that bit in the long grass as you crouched, waiting for the right moment to go over the wall; there was something else that stung, perhaps as you waited, spying, in the bushes. Your heart beat with excitement all the short night. Only at first light was there a chill, the air clear like water.

And in this clear morning light you sauntered into the kitchen, you said, casual, 'You know there's a house, it's up past the cemetery, where there's rich people live? It's got greenhouses.'

My aunt was in the kitchen just then. She was pouring cornflakes into a dish and as she looked up some flakes spilled. She glanced at my mother, and some secret passed between them, in the flick of an eyelid, a twist at the corner of the mouth. 'She means the Hathaways',' my mother said. 'Don't talk about that.' She sounded almost coaxing. 'It's bad enough without little girls talking.'

'What's bad . . .' I was asking, when my mother flared up like a gas-jet: 'Is that where you've been? I hope you've not been up there with Mary Joplin. Because if I see you playing with Mary Joplin, I'll skin you alive. I'm telling you now, and my word is my bond.'

'I'm not up there with Mary,' I lied fluently and fast. 'Mary's poorly.'

'What with?'

I said the first thing that came into my head. 'Ringworm.'

My aunt snorted with laughter.

'Scabies. Nits. Lice. Fleas.' There was pleasure in this sweet embroidery.

'None of that would surprise me one bit,' my aunt said.

'The only thing would surprise me was if Sheila Joplin kept the little trollop at home a single day of her life. I tell you, they live like animals. They've no bedding, do you know?'

'At least animals leave home,' my mam said. 'The Joplins never go. There just gets more and more of them living in a heap and scrapping like pigs.'

'Do pigs fight?' I said. But they ignored me. They were rehearsing a famous incident before I was born. A woman out of pity took Mrs Joplin a pan of stew and Mrs Joplin, instead of a civil no-thank-you, spat in it.

My aunt, her face flushed, re-enacted the pain of the woman with the stew; the story was fresh as if she had never told it before. My mother chimed in, intoning, on a dying fall, the words that ended the tale: 'And so she ruined it for the poor soul who had made it, and for any poor soul who might want to eat it after.'

Amen. At this coda, I slid away. Mary, as if turned on by the flick of a switch, stood on the pavement, scanning the sky, waiting for me.

'Have you had your breakfast?' she asked.

'No.'

No point asking after Mary's. 'I've got money for toffees,' I said.

If it weren't for the persistence of this story about Sheila Joplin and the stew, I would have thought, in later life, that I had dreamed Mary. But they still tell it in the village and laugh about it; it's become unfastened from the original disgust. What a good thing, that time does that for us. Sprinkles us with mercies like fairy dust.

I had turned, before scooting out that morning, framed in the kitchen door. 'Mary's got fly-strike,' I'd said. 'She's got maggots.'

My aunt screamed with laughter.

August came and I remember the grates standing empty, the tar boiling on the road, and fly strips, a glazed yellow studded plump with prey, hanging limp in the window of the corner shop. Each afternoon thunder in the distance, and my mother saying 'It'll break tomorrow,' as if the summer were a cracked bowl and we were under it. But it never did break. Heat-struck pigeons scuffled down the street. My mother and my aunt claimed, 'Tea cools you down,' which was obviously not true, but they swigged it by the gallon in their hopeless belief. 'It's my only pleasure,' my mother said. They sprawled in deck chairs, their white legs stuck out. They held their cigarettes tucked back in their fists like men, and smoke leaked between their fingers. People didn't notice when you came or went. You didn't need food; you got an iced-lolly from the shop: the freezer's motor whined.

I don't remember my treks with Mary Joplin, but by five o'clock we always ended, whatever loop we traced, nearby the Hathaways' house. I do remember the feel of my forehead resting against the cool stone of the wall, before we vaulted it. I remember the fine grit in my sandals, how I emptied it out but then there it was again, ground into the soles of my feet. I remember the leather feel of the leaves in the shrubbery where we dug in, how their gauntleted fingers gently explored my face. Mary's conversation droned in my ear: so me dad says, so me mam says . . . It was at dusk, she promised, it was at twilight, that the comma, which she swore was human, would show itself. Whenever I tried to read a book, this summer, the print blurred. My mind shot off across the fields; my mind caressed the shape of Mary, her grinning mouth, her dirty face, her blouse shooting up over her chest and showing her dappled ribs. She seemed to me full of shadows, exposed where she should not be, but then suddenly tugging down her sleeve, shying from a touch, sulking if you jogged her with your elbow: flinching. Her conversation dwelt, dully, on fates that could befall you; beatings, twistings, flayings. I could only think of the thing she was going to show me. And I had prepared my defence in advance, my defence in case I was seen flitting across the fields. I was out punctuating, I would say. I was out punctuating, looking for a comma. Just by myself and not at all with Mary Joplin.

So I must have stayed late enough, buried in the bushes, for I was drowsy and nodding. Mary jolted me with her elbow; I sprang awake, my mouth dry, and I would have cried out except she slapped her paw across my mouth. 'Look.' The sun was lower, the air mild. In the house, a lamp had been switched on beyond the long windows. One of them opened, and we watched: first one half of the window: a pause: and then the other. Something nudged out into our sight: it was a long chair on wheels, a lady pushing it. It ran easily, lightly, over the stone flags, and it was the lady who drew my attention; what lay on the chair seemed just a dark, shrouded shape, and it was her crisp flowered frock that took my eye, the tight permed shape of her head; we were not near enough to smell her, but I imagined that she wore scent, eau de cologne. The light from the house seemed to dance with her, buoyant, out on to the terrace. Her mouth moved; she was speaking, smiling, to the inert bundle that she pushed. She set the chair down, positioning it carefully, as if on some mark she knew. She glanced about her, turning up her cheek to the mellow, sinking light, then bent to coax over the bundle's head another layer, some coverlet or shawl: in this weather?

'See how she wraps it,' Mary mouthed at me.

I saw; saw also the expression on Mary's face, which was greedy and lost, both at once. With a final pat to the blankets, the lady turned, and we heard the click of her heels on the paving as she crossed to the French window, and melted into the lamp-light.

'Try and see in. Jump up,' I urged Mary. She was taller than I was. She jumped, once, twice, three times, thudding down each time with a little grunt; we wanted to know what was inside the house. Mary wobbled to rest; she crumpled back to her knees; we would settle for what we could get; we studied the bundle, laid out for our inspection. Its shape, beneath the blankets, seemed to ripple; its head, shawled, was vast, pendant. It is like a comma, she is right: its squiggle of a body, its lolling head.

'Make a noise at it, Mary,' I said.

'I dursn't,' she said.

So it was I who, from the safety of the bushes, yapped like a dog. I saw the pendent head turn, but I could not see a face; and at the next moment, the shadows on the terrace wavered, and from between the ferns in their great china pots stepped the lady in the flowered dress, and shaded her eyes, and looked straight at us, but did not see. She bent low over the bundle, the long cocoon, and spoke: she glanced up as if assessing the angle of the dying sun: she stepped back, setting her hands on the handles of the chaise, and with a delicate rocking motion she manoeuvred it, swayed back and angled it, setting it to rest so that the comma's face was raised to the last warmth; at the same time, bending again and whispering, she drew back the shawl.

And we saw — nothing; we saw something not yet become; we saw something, not a face but perhaps, I thought, when I thought about it later, perhaps a negotiating position for a face, perhaps a loosely imagined notion of a face, like God's when he was trying to form us; we saw a blank, we saw a sphere, it was without feature, it was without meaning, and its flesh seemed to run from the bone. I put my hand over my mouth and cowered, shrinking, to my knees. 'Quiet, you.' Mary's fist lashed out at me. She caught me painfully. Mechanical tears, jerked out by the blow, sprang into my eyes.

But when I had rubbed them away I rose up, curiosity like a fish-hook through my gut, and saw the comma was alone on the terrace. The lady had stepped back into the house. I whispered to Mary, 'Can it talk?' I understood, I fully understood now, what my mother had meant when she said at the house of the rich it was bad enough. To harbour a creature like that! To be kind to the comma, to wrap it in blankets . . . Mary said, 'I'm going to throw a stone at it, then we'll see can it talk.'

She slid her hand into her pocket, and what she slid out again was a large, smooth pebble, as if fresh from the seashore, the strand. She didn't find that here, so she must have come prepared. I like to think I put a hand on her wrist, that I said, 'Mary . . .' But perhaps not. She rose from her hiding place, gave a single whoop, and loosed the pebble. Her aim was good, almost good. We heard the pebble ping from the frame of the chair, and at once a low cry, not like a human voice, like something else.

'I bloody got it,' Mary said. For a moment she stood tall and glowing. Then she ducked, she plummeted, rustling, beside me. The evening shapes of the terrace, serene, then fractured and split. With a rapid step the lady came, snapping through the tall arched shadows thrown back by the garden against the house, the shadow of gates and trellises, the rose arbours with their ruined roses. Now the dark flowers on her frock had blown their petals and bled out into the night. She ran the few steps towards the wheeled chair, paused for a split second, her hand fluttering over the comma's head; then she flicked her head back to the house and bawled, her voice harsh, 'Fetch a torch!' That harshness shocked me, from a throat I had thought would coo like a dove, like a pigeon; but then she turned again, and the last thing I saw before we ran was how she bent over the comma, and wrapped the shawl, so tender, about the lamenting skull.

In September Mary was not at school. I expected to be in her class now, because I had gone up and although she was ten it was known that Mary never went up, just stuck where she was. I didn't ask about her at home, because now that the sun was in for the winter and I was securely sealed in my skin I knew it would hurt to have it pulled off, and my mother, as she had said, was a woman of her word. If your skin is off, I thought, at least they look after you. They lull you in blankets on a terrace and speak softly to you and turn you to the light. I remembered the greed on Mary's face, and I partly understood it, but only partly. If you spent your time trying to understand what happened when you were eight and Mary Joplin was ten, you'd waste your productive years in plaiting barbed wire.

A big girl told me, that autumn, 'She went to another school.'

'Reform?'

'What?'

'Is it a reform school?'

'Nah, she's gone to daft school.' The girl slobbered her tongue out, lolled it slowly from side to side. 'You know?'

'Do they slap them every day?'

The big girl grinned. 'If they can be bothered. I expect they shaved her head. Her head was crawling.'

I put my hand to my own hair, felt the lack of it, the chill, and in my ear a whisper, like the whisper of wool; a shawl around my head, a softness like lambswool: a forgetting.

It must have been twenty-five years. It could have been thirty. I don't go back much: would you? I saw her in the street, and she was pushing a buggy, no baby in it, but a big bag with a spill of dirty clothes coming out; a baby tee-shirt with a whiff of sick, something creeping like a tracksuit cuff, the corner of a soiled sheet. At once I thought, well, there's a sight to gladden the eye, one of that lot off to the launderette! I must tell my mum, I thought. So she can say, wonders will never cease.

But I couldn't help myself. I followed close behind her and I said, 'Mary Joplin?'

She pulled the buggy back against her, as if protecting it, before she turned: just her head, her gaze inching over her shoulder, wary. Her face, in early middle age, had become indefinite, like wax: waiting for a pinch and a twist to make its shape. It passed through my mind, you'd need to have known her well to know her now, you'd need to have put in the hours with her, watching her sideways. Her skin seemed swagged, loose, and there was nothing much to read in Mary's eyes. I expected, perhaps, a pause, a hyphen, a space, a space where a question might follow . . . Is that you, Kitty? She stooped over her buggy, and settled her laundry with a pat, as if to reassure it. Then she turned back to me, and gave me a bare acknowledge-ment: a single nod, a full stop.

## ROBERT EDRIC

# Moving Day

'I T MAKES NO sense,' Miller said absently.

He stood at the high window with his back to the two men, and as he spoke he looked down over the level expanse beneath him. The cheap protective screen had long since lost its adhesion and hung in strips from the glass. Looking out now, it sometimes seemed to Miller as though he was watching a slowly blistering film, a gauze of darkening green in which bubbles of vivid and disturbing clarity came and went.

'Why does it *need* to make sense?' the man at the door asked him.

His name was Proctor. Miller remembered him from forty years earlier. They had been boys together, had attended the same school. But Proctor, if he too remembered, remembered only vaguely, and was clearly unwilling to commit himself to the uncertain and dangerous terrain of any distant memory he and Miller might have shared.

'Or, more to the point, why do *you* need it to make sense?' the second, younger man said.

Miller imagined their knowing glances behind his back, this motionless high-five of shared cleverness. He didn't know this second man, but he knew by the way the two of them had so far behaved during their brief visit, that he was some kind of trainee, an apprentice perhaps, and that of the pair of them, he would be the one with most to prove, the one who might want to stamp his mark most forcibly on these otherwise ridiculous and predictable proceedings.

The ice in Miller's glass had almost melted, and he spun what remained of the cubes in the last of the liquid.

'Well?' the apprentice said, then waited scarcely a heartbeat before saying to Proctor, 'He can't answer us, he hasn't got an answer. I thought he was meant to be somebody, thought he was supposed to have big ideas, all the answers. That's what it said in his file. Big man. Somebody. Once.'

Proctor said nothing for a few moments.

The apprentice made a sound as though he might have been spitting dust from his mouth.

'Something like that,' Proctor said eventually, the resignation and weariness in his voice directed at both Miller and his companion in equal measure.

Still without turning to face them, Miller levelled his gaze at one of the holes in his pockmarked screen and focussed on the line of the distant horizon, on the array of smoking towers there, their dark effluent spilling upwards into the sky like ink poured into water, rising vigorously at first, and then slowing, billowing and spreading as the force of expulsion was lost, and as the particles of whatever they were burning today rose through the discoloured and overheated air.

'*Do* you want to say anything?' Proctor asked him. 'You have the right of appeal. I have all the necessary forms.' He started to click at the pad hidden in his palm.

Miller finally turned to face the two men.

'Can I see?' he asked Proctor, who handed the pad to him.

'It's crap,' the apprentice said. 'We're still waiting for the forty-seven.'

'What is it, the forty?' Miller asked Proctor.

'Something like that. Probably nearer thirty. Budget realignments.'

'I heard,' Miller said, handing the pad back.

'Tell me about it,' the apprentice said, unhappy at his exclusion from even this brief exchange. He shook his head and laughed at what he'd said, expecting both Miller and Proctor to somehow signal their agreement.

'*He*'s the thinker,' Proctor said to Miller, who raised his empty glass to the man.

'To thinkers,' Miller said.

And the apprentice, uncertain of the nature of this salute, of the mockery it might contain, drew himself apart from the two older men by saying, 'Yeah, well, we're here because we've got a job to do. Do you want to see our authorization? Does he want to see our authorization?'

'You must be very proud,' Miller said to him.

'What's he talking about?' the apprentice said, pushed even further from them. He was sweating in the no-air-con room, and moisture formed into a near perfect line low on his brow. A solitary bead moved slowly around his left eye and caught in the downy hair of his cheek.

A fly flew across the small apartment and tapped against the glass as though testing it for a flaw, searching for an escape. Outside, it would be dead in seconds; it was why they had moved indoors.

There was a rhyme Miller's grandmother had recited to him, something else he hadn't heard for those same forty years. A fly and a flea were caught in a flue. Said the fly,

'Let us flee,' said the flea, 'Let us fly,' so they flew through a flaw in the flue.

It was why the flies had moved indoors, why they lived, bred, multiplied and died there. Miller swept them into drifts along the bottom of the glass. They were the new dust. There was still the old dust, of course, old dust, old dirt, old stains and detritus, but now there was this other layer, something else to clear away, this stratum of corpses.

Miller wondered how many millennia would pass before the bodies, these new black outlines to every faded and exhausted colour, settled, compacted, solidified and then rose in sheer ebony cliffs out of the shrinking seas; or until they compacted and solidified and sank beneath the empty surface only to be discovered, excavated and burned as fuel in the towers on the horizon.

He smiled at the thought. It was late in the morning. Ten years had passed since he'd stopped counting the drinks he drank, since he'd measured or guessed at the contents of the glasses. Ten years since he'd last wondered about the true nature of the addiction the glasses fed. No one drank in public any more. There was no public. Only the drink. Only the drink and the men like Miller with their needs.

He watched the fly for a moment, saw it fall more and more frequently to the ground as it repeated its instinctive and killing journey towards the light.

Proctor also watched the insect, the two men lost in their shared reverie of what might once have been considered curiosity, wonder almost.

At the door, the apprentice coughed to break the silence, drawing them back to him, away from the dangerous border of their drifting thoughts.

'I'll ask you again,' he said. 'Why do you think it makes no sense?'

In the beginning—not the beginning—in the beginning before the towers and the ever-changing but permanent haze—in that beginning—it had been possible to see the mountains which once formed the beckoning horizon, their already smooth and empty slopes rising to evenly spaced and symmetrical peaks. People had visited them, had been told the tales of the men who had once climbed to their summits.

The peaks had been much higher then, and most had been visible from their foothills. There had always been cloud cover—cloudy *days*, the records showed—implying other days, longer perhaps, when there had been no cloud at all.

And even when the peaks had been obscured, the pictures showed that this cloud had been white and broken, that individual clouds had drifted across the sky. People had given names to these—had named them for what they were—their shape, height, density; and had named them, too, for the objects and creatures they occasionally represented. Just as they had once imposed that same mix of familiarity and awe on the night-time constellations far beyond.

As a small boy Miller had seen the mountains, had been taken there by his father and shown the start of the gentle slopes reaching upwards. But even then the peaks had been lost to him, already something only to be imagined as they rose unseen through the slowly descending haze.

He still possessed an image of his grandfather and his grandfather's brother standing side by side at some point on their climb.

He was interrupted in these loosely assembled thoughts

by the apprentice who, measuring his paces across the room, came to stand beside him at the window.

'Nice view,' the man said, making his true meaning clear. He picked at the peeling screen with his fingernail. 'If I were you —' He stopped abruptly, remembering his purpose there.

'If you were me, what?' Miller asked him.

The man fumbled for something to say. 'If I were you, I'd keep my eyes covered. You forget how dangerous things are.'

Miller resisted saying, 'Things?' The list was too long. The man would have been reciting them for an hour.

'Thanks for the warning,' Miller said.

The man was seldom thanked — seldom even noticed in the presence of his superior — and he was embarrassed by this casual gratitude.

Usually, Miller imagined, Proctor would have done all the talking, with the apprentice beside him nodding and repeating key words in emphasis and support.

But today was different.

Perhaps Proctor, too, understood that. And perhaps he, too, had known of the mountains and those other clouds. Perhaps he, too, had heard tales from his own grandparents.

'How far?' Miller said to him. He left his place at the window and went to the bottle on the table. He offered it to Proctor, who looked at it for a few seconds and then declined the offer.

*You should have come alone*, Miller thought. He poured himself another drink.

'How far what?' Proctor said, already guessing.

'To the mountains.'

'What mountains?' the apprentice said, looking from one man to the other.

Proctor took several steps towards the window and looked out. He removed his dark glasses and blinked in the unaccustomed glare, easing the ache from his eyes between his forefinger and thumb.

'Thirty-five K,' he said. 'It's thirty-five K. To the nearest. *Was* thirty-five K.'

The apprentice looked at him in surprised disbelief.

*Heresy*, Miller thought, and smiled. He raised his glass to Proctor and nodded once.

'Thirty-five K to what?' the apprentice said, his voice rising. 'What mountains? What are you talking about? You surely don't—' He stopped talking. After a moment, he began to tap the pad in his own palm.

'What are you doing?' Proctor asked him, his unshielded eyes still on the view below.

'We're supposed to log all the dimensions,' the younger man said.

'Nothing will have changed.'

'It's why we're here. Remember? Why we're here. Miller?' He followed this with a succession of serial numbers, every one of which felt to Miller like a finger prodded into his chest. 'Reallocation, remember? He *was* three. Now he's one. Miller.' He repeated the first of the numbers.

Ten years had passed since Miller had been three. The longest years of his life. Ten years during which everything had been stripped from him as painfully and as completely as though it were his own flesh.

'He's right,' he said to Proctor. 'I *was* three; now I'm one.'

'It means—' the apprentice began.

'He *knows* what it means,' Proctor said sharply, causing the man to fall silent.

Miller sipped at his new drink, screwing his eyes at the sharpness of the spirit after the diluted tastelessness of the last. *You, too*, he thought, careful to avoid looking at Proctor, who finally replaced his dark glasses and turned his back on the distant view.

'You'll have to relocate,' Proctor said. 'Sorry.'

*After ten years?* Miller thought. *Why now?*

'The decision was nothing to do with us,' the apprentice said. 'And when he says "Sorry" he in no way suggests or implies personal determination or liability.'

'Of course,' Miller said, more to Proctor than to reassure his companion. *Determination?* he thought. *When did that particular word alter its meaning in their favour?*

There were seventeen floors of apartments above him and twenty-six below. Forty four floors. Forty-eight apartments on each. Two thousand, one hundred and twelve apartments. At least one thousand, seven hundred of which were empty, half of them uninhabitable. The top ten floors had been the first to be abandoned, followed by the subterranean and ground-floor levels.

But it was a matter of simple calculation. He was deemed to live in a space adequate and appropriate for three people. Legally, he knew, he had been a trespasser or squatter these past ten years. And because of everything else that had happened to him during that time, it gratified Miller to think of himself as one or both of those things. A man between the start and the finish of something, a man without maps, a man in limbo, a man waiting, a man without expectation or hope.

'Do you know how many empty apartments there are in this tower?' he said, mostly to himself.

'That has nothing to do with why we're here,' the apprentice said quickly, the same smug note in his voice.

And for the first time, Miller found himself angry at the

man and wanted to tell him to shut up, to shut up or to grow up or to leave. He wanted to throw his drink, or his drink and the glass which held it, at the man. He wanted to grab him and push him against the glass, watch him hit it and fall back into the room, fall to his hands and knees on the hard floor in front of him; grab the man and push him against the glass and watch it shatter and break and then watch the man fall through it, struggling to regain some lost measure of balance for the first time in his life and fumbling to hold on to the cascade of shattered pieces through which he was so suddenly falling into the warm air outside, and then as he began his flailing, wide-eyed descent to the ground below. To the all too solid ground below, where his body would land and where all uncertainty would be extinguished in an instant. Just as it had been extinguished for Miller all those years ago.

'Did you hear what I said?' the man said to him. 'I said, the vacancy-opportunity of the apartments specific to this tower has nothing whatsoever to do with why we're here today.'

'I heard you,' Miller said. 'My apologies.'

The apprentice looked to Proctor for his support, for him to say something that might indicate to Miller that he had resumed his own exact and prescribed role in these proceedings.

'You were three,' Proctor said. He reached out his hand, as though he was going to touch Miller, clasp his arm perhaps, let him know he understood and sympathised. But the gesture was beyond him — forbidden, anyway — and so he drew back his hand, looking at it briefly before letting it fall to his side.

'And now I'm one,' Miller said, the words yet another of their unspoken apologies.

'At last,' the apprentice said. 'Shall we move on? You're not the only relocation we're docketed for this morning.'

The solitary fly was back at the window, tapping haphazardly against the glass level with the apprentice's head, and Miller was momentarily distracted by this and watched the creature closely.

'What?' the apprentice said, imagining *he* was the focus of Miller's gaze and unspoken thoughts. 'What?'

It was another beginning—a time before the first ending, before the last decade—before the upper floors had finally been abandoned to the heat and the dust, and when the inhabitants of the higher apartments had congregated on the walled roof of the tower. It was where the air-conditioning shafts with their faltering fans rose into the dusty air. It was where people took out chairs and small tables, where they brought food and drink and gathered together to toast the hazy sunrises and sunsets—yet another near-forgotten ceremony, more impulse than understanding, to which they still clung.

Often, and increasingly as the years passed, and as the intermittent operation of the distant towers became continuous, these gatherings were interrupted and curtailed by the storms of dust which drove everyone indoors. It was the same storms—and the winds which now lasted between them—that had finally emptied the upper floors.

Sometimes, these storms rose in gentle currents; and sometimes they arrived with a fierce and unforeseeable rush, catching those on the high roof unawares. People were blown off their feet; the lighter of the tables and chairs were blown against the restraining walls; glasses, crockery and bottles were smashed. A woman was blown against one of the vents and badly injured.

That had been during the fiercest of their storms, and

at the time the people up on the roof had all spoken of it as a freak occurrence.

Afterwards, there had been a lull of almost a month when no further storms had arrived, and when the weather, though still overheated at ground level, had been almost balmy and calm up on the roof.

And then, as the year passed from high into low summer, the storms had come again, one after the other, first ten, then twenty, then a hundred, one after the other, and each one seemingly longer and more ferocious than the one before it.

A time had passed; a new time had started.

It was when the Miller who had been three had become the Miller who was one.

He had not actually seen what had happened to his wife and daughter — he had turned away from them to rub the stinging from his eyes — but he had been standing only a few metres from them. And one moment they had been standing close to him, eating, drinking, talking and laughing, and the next moment they were gone. No longer standing with him, no longer eating or drinking or talking or laughing, but gone. And he had not known then what a lifetime the word encompassed, what unfathomed depths and unravellings, what inconsolable agonies still lay ahead.

Gone. Just as the details of his waiting and then searching and then terrible imaginings had now gone from him in the broken reflections of his glasses and his bottles, and in the melting ice and the insulated near-double images of his window with its blistering, shrinking view of everything beyond.

When it was over, and after the apprentice had finished tapping the required information into his palm set and had gone to wait in the relative cool of the internal corridor, Proctor turned to Miller and said, 'I remember.'

*Remember what?* Miller thought. *The mountains? The sky before the smoke- and dust-filled haze? Your own distant and evaporated family? What? My own lost wife and daughter? Me, Miller, Miller when three? You remember what?*

'I know you do,' Miller said. It was probably a crime for the man to have admitted even that little.

For years afterwards, he had woken with a start from the dream of his beautiful wife and young daughter flying through the air like vigorous birds on strong wings, while he, Miller, too afraid to leap and fly with them, could only watch as they grew ever smaller in their circling orbits; woken, too, from the nightmare of their uncomprehending plummet to the ground, sucked into the debris-filled vortex of that same wind which had cast them from the rooftop and left him completely alone with the dust in his eyes and without the faintest notion, in that solitary, ignorant instant, of what had happened.

'No, I *remember*,' Proctor insisted.

Like the apprentice before him, Miller wanted to tell him to shut up, not to tell him what he remembered—him, Miller, the man who remembered everything, who forgot nothing, however hard he tried—to shut up and to leave, to join the man fanning himself with his hand in the corridor outside.

Instead, he said, 'Tell me.'

And at that single, gentle prompt, Proctor said, 'Cirrostratus, cirrocumulus, cirrus, cumulonimbus, altostratus, altocumulus, nimbostratus, cumulus, stratocumulus, stratus.'

They were the names of the lost clouds in their proper order, starting at height and reaching down to the ground, invisible in near-space, invisible in the fogs and mists and hazes they formed. And Miller remembered them too, remembered the forgotten rote of their names, remembered their extinction in the smoke and the dust, these lazy and uncaring erasers drawn over those clear blue skies, obliterating the clouds for ever and without even the faintest murmur of regret from the men and women below.

Proctor repeated the names, mesmerized by what he'd retrieved, and this time, Miller joined him, the two men word- and emphasis-perfect in their shared mantra, smiles on their faces, their eyes closed, boys together, conducting themselves with the vague and liquid movement of their fingers, and hearing somewhere in the room, somewhere across the forty years which at once divided and connected them, the muted time-keeping tapping of the solitary fly as it resumed its own unstoppable journey into the light that had for so long remained beyond its reach.

# Tristram and Isolde

W E G O T B A C K later than we expected, after the shops shut, but we didn't fret. Everything in the flat had been left ready for us: a cardboard box of dry groceries on the kitchen counter, the fridge stocked with vegetables, milk and wine, the sitting room tidied and vacuumed, and a pile of ironed blue sheets in the cupboard. No radio mumbling, no TV flickering with the sound turned down. The place felt full of echoes. Empty. We would both have to grow larger to fill it.

Inhabiting the space with him alone made me inventive. I wanted to try out new gestures, new routes between cooker and cupboard and shelf. I crossed the kitchen floor with a dancer's steps, twirling to the ping of the microwave. We curled on the sofa together, his arm around me, and ate cashew nuts from the bowl in my lap. He poured some wine and I shared it with him, though I don't much like wine. What mattered was taking a sip from his glass. We toasted one another. Izzy, my darling, he sighed.

We slept in each other's arms all night long, my head tucked between his shoulder and chin, my legs wrapped around his. I woke from time to time, in between dreams, to feel his breath, warm and regular, brush my cheek; to feel his heartbeat. His smooth skin smelt of fresh soap, and cashew nuts, and mushrooms. We'd eaten mushrooms, black and buttery, for supper. Now their juices scented his sweat. As morning bladed the curtains, he began to stir, holding me even closer. Still half asleep, I laid my face against the soft fur curling across his breast and stroked it. I encircled his waist. I held onto him and caressed him. Eyes shut, I whispered: don't go back there. I don't want you to go. I want you to stay with me. I nuzzled him, licked him, bit him gently. I said: I'm going to tie you to me with a silk ribbon, then you won't be able to leave me. Not ever. He pinched my chin and said: so you'll have to come with me then, won't you? He kissed me all over my face and I kissed him back. Together we kicked off the quilt and rolled out of bed.

I brushed my hair in front of the bathroom mirror. He liked to plunge his hands into my mop of curls, twiddle them between his fingers, rummage them about. He liked to pretend to lift me up by the tops of my ears. He said I had pointed ears, like an elf. This morning, though, we didn't play those games. He sat in the bath, knees up, whistling, while I scrubbed his golden-brown back with the string mitt well soaped with the green soap I'd given him for his birthday. We both disliked perfumed soap. This one, egg-shaped, was made with olive oil but just smelled very clean. I liked smells, but not the sickly-sweet variety. I liked the smell of newly cut grass, bracken in hot sun, salt-crusted pebbles on the beach, creosote, fish frying, newly painted walls. Most of all I loved the way his skin smelt of what he'd just eaten. If he'd been out without me to a restaurant I could always tell, when he came home and cuddled me, what he'd had for dinner. I shut my eyes, held him tight, and sniffed him. Sometimes he smelt of lemons, sometimes of blue cheese. He didn't eat a lot of meat but if he did it came off him in a strong red whiff and I felt a wolf was hugging me.

While he talked on the phone I made breakfast. Saturday morning alone together: a feast. I decided to lay the table with the best plates, the pale-pink ones that gleamed like satin. I spread the blue-and-white checked tablecloth, cut bread for toast and made a pot of tea, put out the butter and the marmalade. We ate porridge sprinkled with brown sugar, and two slices each of brown toast. Then he washed up while I swept the floor, shook the cloth and put the rubbish out. We locked the front door and set off. I'd tied him to me with a length of string I found in the kitchen drawer, the one where we kept matches and bits of greaseproof paper and odd nails and screws. I knotted one end around his right wrist. You see, I said: I wasn't joking. Now you can't run away and leave me. He pulled on his leash and jumped up and down and growled. He pawed me and pretended to lick my nose. Then we walked along hand in hand. Love, like sap, a green juice, coursed from his heart down his arm through our joined hands up my arm into my heart and I felt so happy I smiled at everyone we met. A bunch of violet pansies had pushed up from under a low front-garden wall and was blooming in a pavement crack. I loved those pansies' courage, daring to be in the wrong place, and I loved the fact nobody had picked them or trampled on them, and I loved his warm palm enclosing mine, holding love there like a gold bead.

Through the alley, onto the concrete bridge over the railway line, past the disused factories, across the graveyard and the wasteland, towards the river. Two hundred yards along the water's edge and we reached our secret place. In through the tall iron gates we went. We curved around a high hedge. The city vanished. No streets or cars. No traffic noise. Just birdsong. Broad paths of scuffed sand, soft under our feet, crisscrossed the tussocky grass. Low hills thick with bracken stretched away in every direction to the horizon's rim. We swam in pale-gold rays and white mist and cold air. Well wrapped up in our jackets and scarves, we lifted our faces to the sun and felt coldness sliding under its heat. Layers of warmth and cold, delicate as a millefeuille. This morning I felt I could eat the whole world, roll it on my tongue crisp as pastry, tart and sweet as oranges.

Dogs trotted past, pursued by their owners. We nosed along like the dogs, in pursuit of our private quarry: more time alone together. The only way to get it was to be ruthless: to run away. To avoid all the mutterers, the finger-waggers, the no-sayers. To blot them out. I didn't much care what they thought but he did. It mattered so much to him that we observed the forms, the decencies. He didn't want to hurt anyone. He wasn't yet ready to tell everybody how much we loved each other. He told me, though, and that was all I cared about.

I untied the string from his wrist. It had got us this far; now I no longer needed it. He was as enchanted as I by the golden day, the fresh smell of earth, the crackle of dry leaves drifting on the cool breeze, the green spaces; they tugged us forwards. We turned off the main path and entered the wood. A series of copses dotting the waving mass of bracken. Horse-chestnuts and beeches and oaks bent towards each other over our heads. We pushed through the waist-high greenery, following the deer tracks, narrow lines opening in the curled fronds that pressed up against our waists as we plunged along. Under our feet we crushed the springy ferns, releasing their sun-warmed, bittersweet scent.

He walked ahead of me because he knew the maze of

tracks better than I did. I followed his dark yellow corduroy back. Deeper and deeper into the wood we went.
Sometimes a jay started up, or a magpie flapped past, or a
lime-green parrot turned over in a tree like a leaf. Doves
and pigeons cooed out of sight. Branches moved far off in
the sea of green, rippling it.

No: not branches but ears pricking up. Green and gold
and brown swaying pools and currents of light coalesced
into deer suddenly visible, raising their delicate necks.
Nearby reared other branches, fierce and forked: horned
antlers. Part of the forest transformed itself into a red stag.
He turned to look at us. On his head he bore his antlers
like a tall crown, a candelabra of bone. All wreathed with
streamers of green fern. He was a stag and he was the king
of the wood. My knees wanted to fold. I wanted to fall
down and put my forehead on the ground and salute him.
I stood very still. He reared his head and hollered. A great
cry wrenched out of him, answered far away: another stag,
invisible, bellowing back.

His herd of female deer stepped out, slender and
stately, sunspotted; rocking forwards silkily like boats.
He marshalled them, kept them together. They didn't
mind our presence; they were used to us, to our hands
empty of weapons. People who knew no better, men
with enormous cameras, crept far too close to the deer,
bothering them, and the stag raised his head and roared,
warning them off. The men with cameras thought they
could possess the deer by taking pictures of them. You
couldn't. They didn't let themselves be captured. They
preferred to flee. The deer swirled with the stag away into
the forest. They melted back into sun-dappled greenery,
they became part of it again and vanished.

We reached our destination: a particular oak tree in the
heart of the plantation. Very tall, with ribbed black bark

framing the entry to its hollow trunk. We had discovered it a year ago; the dark interior invited us to climb in. Our secret room. Inside, we stood packed together, a close fit; a double vein of green sap. Two green stems plaited together. My face against his jacket, our hands in each other's pockets. You're the green man, I whispered: and I'm the green woman. Like the chapter in Tristram and Isolde where they run away together into the forest and live there secretly. To myself I whispered: we're married now, I've tied you to me, I've knotted us together for ever and ever. I knew, of course, that like Tristram he was married to someone else, Iseult of the white hands, queen of the kitchen in her white rubber gloves, but that didn't matter. I was his real wife, the one he secretly loved best. She wasn't here now, was she? She was far away and she couldn't see what we were doing.

He took the length of string out of my pocket and twined it into a circle and crowned me with it. His arms hugged me round. He said: we're very attached to each other, aren't we! Laughing. I breathed him in: ferns and sweat and soap and tea.

We clambered out of the hollow trunk, squinting in the sunlight, brushing bits of bark off ourselves. We climbed up the tree. He made his joined hands into a ladder step for me and tossed me up onto the lowest branch. I caught it and swung myself up and he came after me. Up and up we went, piercing into greenness, rustling sun-burnished leaves beneath us and above us and all around us. Well hidden now: no one would ever find us here. The deer passing below might scent us, the ants zigzagging along branches run over us, the pigeons perch on us, but no human being would ever guess our presence. We'd climbed out of the human world and vanished into the heavens. Our sky-kingdom; just him and myself and the beating heart of the tree. He sat astride one branch, his back against the main trunk of the oak, and I straddled another a little higher up, swinging my booted feet back and forth over his knees. For a long time we sat like that, listening to the sounds of the wood, not speaking. From time to time he reached up with his hand and grasped my boot and gave it a little punch and pushed it gently to and fro.

The warmth of the sun deepened under my jacket, my skin. My thoughts floated like leaves rafting down. We could live here as long as we chose. We could gather dry branches and twigs for fires. For food we could roast acorns and chestnuts, nibble grass and the soft tips of ferns, shoot foxes and pigeons and squirrels. Either we'd sleep in the forked branches of the tree or else we'd make a bed of bracken under it. We could weave the bracken into green camouflage coats to hide us when we went hunting. We could stick feathers into our hair to disguise ourselves as birds. Nobody would ever find us, however long they searched, because we'd hide so high up in the tree. We'd hold our breath when the searchers came past: they'd never guess what strange creatures nested between tree-top and blue sky. He and I together made one single creature of shared love, shared thoughts, hands clasped, eyes fastened together, we completed each other, we were enough, we were all we needed, we belonged together and would never part.

I told him all this inside my mind. I didn't need to talk it out in words. I poured my love into him and he poured his into me, we were a single flow of sweetness that went back and forth. Time stopped, didn't matter; our green world held us. The tree's green arms. Just we two, our circle, in drowsy golden light and warmth.

He shouted. The world broke in two and the fragments flying apart hit me in the face, in the mouth, in the teeth. I put my hands over my face to protect myself from arrowing shattered glass. He shouted: fuck just look at the time! I couldn't speak, couldn't look at him. He cried: come on, Izzy darling, time to go, I'll give you a hand down. The sky blunted my open mouth. I hated him so much I swayed and rocked, nearly fainted.

Lovers have to part. Lovers have to snatch the time when they can meet. Lovers don't have long enough together. Lovers complain and grumble and cry.

Especially secret lovers. Outlaw lovers. We could float in our green treetop world outside time and feel free there, but sooner or later a mobile would bleep and summon us back to streets and hospital wards and that wrinkled grub in the white plastic cot next to her bed. I grizzled, stomping along behind him. He grabbed my hand and towed me back into the street, towards the bus stop. He put on a fake charming voice so that all the old ladies on the bus would think aaah what a good father he is. You want to see Mummy, don't you, Izzy darling? And your new little brother? Of course you do. Last night they were both so tired but this morning they'll give you a big smile. And you'll give them one back, won't you?

Sooner or later people came and caught you and you were found out and punished. It was your fault. What you'd imagined was too terrible ever to be mentioned so you just buried it in the hollow trunk of the oak tree under a heap of leaves where it could rot and be forgotten about and you were the oak tree hollow inside nothing inside you but a secret going bad going more rotten by the day emptiness powdery dry and grey as ash.

Mummy said: did you find the frozen pizzas, love?

I kicked the leg of the baby's cot, jiggling it, and the baby woke up and started to howl. The cry wrapped itself around my ribs like ribbons drawn tight threatening to stop my breathing.

Sunshine fell onto the white cream paint of the windowsill, as it did in the kitchen at home where, a black bulk against the light, she spent so much time bending at the sink, her back to me, the radio on the shelf chitter-chattering.

Now Mummy leaned over, picked up the baby, fastened it to her breast. She said to Daddy: did you remember to bring the video camera, darling?

The metal window, pushed open, let in cool air to the hospital room. I breathed out so hard that the ribbons binding me broke and I leaped high up in the air and became invisible, I leaped up to the windowsill, balanced, concentrated then jumped, flew out, across the city streets down towards the river the bridge back into the green park. I landed softly. I trotted fast along the tracks, swerving into the green-gold bracken to avoid dogs and walkers, I made towards the woods. In dappled light, whiteness playing with darkness, dancing and overlapping, I could merge with the waving bronze undergrowth, become apparent, dissolve again, and so I became my new, true self, hoisting my antler coronet wreathed with ferns, bearing it with lightness and grace, calling to my deer to surround me then vanishing with them into the heart of the forest.

# DAI VAUGHAN

# Looted

'THE SMELL OF death is high explosive smoke and powdered granite.' It's the laconic tone that makes that sentence stay in the mind, he thinks: a sentence from Hemingway's commentary to the film *Spanish Earth*. And true now as ever, Eric tells himself as he moves slowly, rifle at the ready, along the broad street whose buildings have slipped like unstable piles of documents to span the pavement and almost block the roadway, impeding traffic. Not that there's much traffic anyhow, just the occasional staff car or Corgi two-stroke or lashed-up rickshaw-hearse . . . Tired, obsolete, meaningless documents which once spelled death or life.

From an opening to his right the faint sound of dislodged grit makes him freeze. Probably only rats or children. There has been no sniper activity for three days; but still, it's too early to make assumptions. The lower storeys of this building seem intact, though as he looks up he can see sky through the higher windows. The glass-paned double doors are smashed and splintered; and he has to step over them to enter the hallway from which the stairs begin their broad spiral ascent. Hugging the wall, he climbs to the first floor landing where the light is already flooding in through the wrecked floorboards above, the staircase ending abruptly in mid-curvature. Two apartments give onto the landing. Both doors are missing, presumably taken for firewood or perhaps for stretchers. The doorway of one is impassably choked with fallen masonry. Eric edges cautiously into the other and finds himself in what was once an elegant living room, sunlight sieved by suspended dust as it must once have been sieved by the shredded lace curtains. There is almost an air of welcome.

Having explored the bedroom, the bathroom, the kitchen, all of which are empty but for a couple of broken stools, every utensil and most of the fittings having already found their way into the barter economy which is the only economy now flourishing, Eric returns to the living room. He finds himself oddly reluctant to leave. What is it? Is it something to do with the proportions — a memory of a room known in childhood? In the centre of the ripped carpet, segments of which have been neatly sliced away presumably for use as rugs, is the bulk of a circular, family-size table, once proudly polished. To judge from its scars it has been attacked with an axe; but whoever was attacking it for some reason left the job unfinished. On the stone mantelpiece sits a cracked glass dome which, he supposes, would once have protected an ormolu clock from the gentle perils of domesticity. To the side of the fireplace, undamaged except by neglect, is a pathetically spindly gilt chair. And above this chair there remains, hung from a small hook, what is evidently a painting, about five inches wide by seven high.

Eric lifts the picture from the wall and knocks the frame lightly with his knuckles to loosen some of the sooty clag which is obscuring the image. It seems to be a landscape of some sort: trees, a vista. On impulse, some impulse of tenderness which he cannot quite identify, he stuffs the thing into his pack. Whatever the reason, he does not feel he can just abandon it there. Later, back in his billet, he sets about trying to clean the surface with cotton wool and lighter fuel. The corporal says he was once told that the way to clean paintings was with slices of onion; so he goes down to the cook-house and begs half an onion, but it doesn't seem to have much effect, and he reverts to his original method. Eventually the image is revealed as an overgrown avenue between two rows of tall trees. In the distance, outlined grey against sunset-tinged sky, is a tall pillar or column on which is hunched the form, presumably a sculpture, of some sort of an animal.

The time comes for his regiment to be shipped back to Blighty; and everyone's kit is checked. When asked where he got the painting, Eric says he bought it in the flea market—just happened to appeal to him, can't really say why . . . He has suddenly realised he could be done for looting. But he is waved through with no further questions; and it soon becomes obvious that it's the idiots who want to sail away home with an unexploded Jerry shell or a Luger with a full clip of ammo whom the authorities are really out to nab.

In the years that follow, this little picture — not so much a finished painting, more what they call a colour sketch — becomes one of Eric's most treasured possessions. In the home where he and Sandra bring up their two sons it hangs, not over the mantel, where he is afraid the updraught of hot air might damage its surface, but to the right of it. It seldom fails to attract the admiring attention of visitors.

Then, one day in the 1970s, he encounters an article in one of the Sunday supplements about valuable paintings which disappeared during the turmoils of war and have not been seen since. One of the accompanying photographs shows a spacious room with a large, circular table in the foreground. Over the fireplace, above an ormolu clock in a glass dome, hangs a large painting identified in the caption as a missing Rembrandt. Another painting, which hangs above a spindly gilt chair to the right, is too small to reveal any detail at that distance; but Eric knows perfectly well what it is. And the room looks so comfortably familiar that he can scarcely believe he saw it only once, and as a ruin. After discussing the pros and cons with Sandra, he writes a letter to the author of the article, c/o the Sunday paper, asking if any information is available about the smaller picture shown in the photograph. But he receives no reply.

Twelve more years have passed when, without forewarning, a letter arrives from a company of solicitors acting for a client in Germany. They wish to send a representative to examine a painting thought to be in Eric's possession. They include a snapshot, of a statuesque woman with coiled plaits and a jet necklace, in the background of which the little painting is clearly visible. They propose a date, and request a reply as a matter of urgency.

'How on earth do they know?' Sandra asks.

'They can't know for certain. But they could have got my name and address from that letter I sent expressing an interest in it. They could have checked through Interpol, or whoever it is you check with, about where I was stationed in the last days of the war: put two and two together . . . It's even possible the army kept a record of my statement about having bought the thing in a flea market.'

'Why don't we just hide the picture and deny all knowledge?'

'What would be the point? We keep it because we

like looking at it—because it's part of our lives. I can't imagine it'd be worth much money, anyway.'

'All the same, perhaps you should stick to your story about the flea market.'

On the agreed day the lawyer, specialist in misattributions, forgeries and general malfeasance in arts-related matters, sits sipping tea in their shabby chair, long legs pinstriped and crossed, shoes glossy and strangely narrow. He has little doubt the painting is the original.

'You didn't by any chance receive a provenance with it?'

'A what?'

'A document listing former sales and ownership.'

'From a flea market?'

'Mm. I suppose not.'

'So—you know who it's by, then?'

'Yes. It's a Böcklin.' Eric looks blank. 'Swiss. Nineteenth century. Not in Rembrandt's bracket, obviously; but of sufficient value for the owners to take the matter of its theft quite seriously.'

'Theft?' Eric lets his annoyance get the better of him. 'Look, those buildings were about to be demolished. They were a public hazard. D'you think the sappers were going to risk their lives hunting through every room in case someone had left a minor masterpiece behind before they set their charges? If I hadn't rescued that painting, it would have been crushed under ten tons of rubble before the week was out.'

'Aha—so you didn't actually buy it at a market stall.' The lawyer allows himself the sort of smile a cut-throat razor might if it could. 'Never mind. Criminal proceedings are not envisaged. You will be hearing from us shortly.'

Some days later they receive a letter advising them to relinquish the painting voluntarily by the end of the month or be prepared to defend their position in court. At first, Eric's sons are all for fighting the case. Why hand our picture over to a bunch of sodding Nazis? But Eric points out that even to win such a case would cost more money than they can spare; and they probably wouldn't win it. They've enjoyed the picture, at no financial outlay, for most of their lives. They should be grateful for that. It doesn't take long for the family to agree. But the younger son remains bitter:

'What gets my goat is that the people who are demanding restitution of that painting aren't people who ever lived with it and felt its loss personally. They're far too young. All they care about is its cash value.'

Shortly after surrendering the Böcklin — for the last fortnight he allowed himself to think of it as 'the Böcklin', as if he had always done so — Eric accepts his firm's offer of early retirement from his post of deputy chief warehouseman. Though still a month or two short of 60, he begins in subtle ways to behave like a pensioner, taking up a succession of more or less inappropriate hobbies. At one point he equips himself with acrylic colours and a proprietary brand of prepared board and begins trying to copy his painting from memory, reasoning that, if he remembers the image as perfectly as he believes he does, he should surely be able to reproduce it. But, while some of his efforts may be good enough to serve as reminders of the original, none captures its magic.

Every once in a while, Eric's elder son treats his ailing parents to a drive in the country. On one such occasion they are visiting a deer park, now owned by the National Trust, which was once attached to a stately home and landscaped by — so the guidebook says — a former journeyman of Capability Brown. They have been exploring the grounds for some three quarters of an hour when Eric suddenly halts. Before him stretches an avenue, somewhat overgrown, between two rows of mature beeches. In the distance beyond them, catching the light of a late autumn afternoon, there rises a weathered limestone column on top of which crouches a carving of an animal of some sort—perhaps a lion, perhaps a dog. The others stroll back to find what has detained him, and he points out the clear resemblance to their lost painting. They sort of see it, sort of don't.

'You're trying to tell us,' his son asks, 'that the painting was a premonition of this moment?'

'No, no; nothing supernatural, like. It's just that . . .'

Just that what?

It seems he has a decision to make. He is being invited to step into this world exactly as he once stepped into that shelled building, once stuffed that painting into his haversack. He feels he has required this of himself. Yet has he not, by surrendering the painting, given up that right? And besides, might he not by entering this land-scape delete the memory of the painting altogether?

Is the very invitation which tantalised him for years now in process of being rescinded? Already the light of memory, somehow unravelling, seems, in slackening its grip from violet to mauve, to have leached from the grey pillar a hint of rose he never quite noticed but is now per-suaded was always there. Perhaps, by turning back now, he can allow the remembered painting to remain as it was—though perhaps it is already too late.

He hesitates. And then his family call him to the car.

## ALISON MOORE

# When the Door Closed, It Was Dark

I N  E N G L A N D ,  I T  will be autumn. She imagines the paling sun and the purifying chill, the bare branches and the fallen leaves and the smell of decomposition, the smell of the end of the summer. She longs for short days and early nights, wanting home and hibernation.

She steps from the concrete slabs on to the iron staircase and begins the climb up. She can hardly bear the weight she is carrying, and the rising sun beats down on her.

She remembers her first sight of this place. The taxi, air-conditioned and smelling of pine trees, pulled away, leaving her standing on the slabs beside the block of flats. The paintwork was bruise-coloured and blistered. The midday heat was terrific. There was one flat on each floor, the higher storeys accessed by the iron staircase which zigzagged up the front of the building like the teeth of her mother's pinking shears or a child's drawing of lightning.

She climbed the four flights up to the flat in which she would be staying, carrying her suitcase in one hand and holding on to the railing with the other. Reaching the top, she wiped the sweat from her face with the palm of her hand and smelt the tang of iron on her skin. She knocked on the door and waited. She thought she could hear the baby squealing or screaming.

The door was opened by a woman wearing black, with her head shaved and her hairline low on her narrow forehead. Offering the woman a damp hand, Tina attempted one of the phrases she had practised in the back of the taxi during the long drive from the airport, even though the family's online advertisement had said, 'Can speak English.'

'I'm Tina,' she said, 'your au pair.'

The woman stabbed at herself with her thumb and said, in her own language, 'Grandmother.'

The shrill noise came again from inside the flat. 'The baby?' asked Tina.

'No,' said Grandmother, and beckoned her inside.

The narrow hallway into which she stepped was packed with sunshine—the wallpaper and the carpet were luridly colourful—but when the door closed, it was dark. She walked down the hallway with the violent patterns unseen beneath her feet, her hand sliding blindly down the wall, the wallpaper rough to the touch, and the screaming filled the hallway.

Climbing the two stone steps up to the kitchen behind Grandmother, she first saw the broad back of a tall man standing beneath a bare lightbulb, and then she saw the pig clamped, shrieking, between his knees. She imagined him leading the pig up the iron staircase, her trotters skidding on the metal steps, and heaving her if she would not climb. She pictured the pig stepping through the front door, on to the brightly patterned carpet, being guided down the dark hallway and up the steps into the kitchen.

Another man was silhouetted against the window. He was sitting on a chest freezer, smoking a cigarette and laughing. Grandmother pointed at him and said, 'Father.'

A baby sat beside him in a high-chair, watching the man with the pig. Tina could tell they were all family — the men and even the baby had the same narrow forehead and the same broad jaw as the woman. They too had black clothes and shaved heads.

Grandmother turned to the man with the pig and said, 'Uncle.' He looked at Tina, looked her in the eye, but did not smile. He returned his attention to the pig squirming between his legs, picked up a large knife, and then he smiled. He wrestled the pig out of the kitchen and across the unlit hallway into a bathroom, and closed the door. The squealing got louder, and then stopped.

All summer, every evening, she has eaten pork.

On the first night, they had chops. They ate together in the kitchen, and Father fed scraps of meat alternately to the baby and to the dog. The family talked quickly, interrupting and raising their voices over one another. The pace and the dialect and the heavy accent made it impossible for Tina to follow the conversation, and her formal phrases were like wallflowers at a wild party.

She must have been staring at Grandmother when Uncle turned to Tina and said in English, 'There was death in the family,' and he touched his shaved scalp to indicate that this was the custom.

'I'm sorry,' she said, and then, 'So you speak English.'

'Yes,' he said, 'I have a girlfriend in England. She lives in London. Where do you live?'

'I'm from Leicester.'

Uncle pushed away his empty plate and said, 'Tigers.'

'Yes,' said Tina, 'Leicester Tigers,' and she smiled, but he did not.

Father lit a cigarette.

She was not due to start work for the family until the

morning. Tired from her journey, Tina excused herself and went to bed early. In the bathroom, the shower curtain was pulled across; she did not pull it back. She washed her face and brushed her teeth quickly, went to her room and shut the door. There was a lock—a keyhole—but no key. Despite the heat, she only half-undressed, and got into bed.

She lay awake for a while, hearing the family talking loudly elsewhere in the house. When she fell asleep, they crept into her dreams—she dreamt that there was someone in her room, standing at the foot of her bed, casting a large shadow on the wall, and the pig was there. It jumped up on to the mattress and lay down, heavy and warm against her body, snorting and snuffling in the dark.

When she woke in the morning, opening her eyes to the strange ceiling, she found that she could not move her legs. She lifted her head and looked down the bed. The dog lay across her shins, nosing noisily at something between its paws. It stayed there watching her with its sad, black eyes, its sopping tongue hanging down, while she dressed, and then it followed her to the kitchen, carrying something in its wet mouth.

In the hallway, she met Uncle and he said, 'Tigers.' She smiled, but he did not.

Grandmother and Father were already in the kitchen when she and Uncle arrived. Tina said, 'Good morning,' sat in the place which had been set for her and looked at the breakfast already on her plate.

'Pig fat,' said Uncle, sitting down to his. 'Eat it.' The dog was chasing a half-eaten snout around the kitchen floor with its nose.

Father lit a cigarette, and Uncle said to Tina, 'You have to clean the bath.' The men left, and Grandmother cleared the table around her, and eventually Tina was alone with the baby. She leaned towards him and said, 'Hello,' first in English and then in his own language. She pulled faces and made animal noises and laughed awkwardly, while the unsmiling baby regarded her.

When the baby was napping in his cot in Grandmother's room, Tina went to the bathroom with Uncle. 'I will show you,' he said, pulling aside the shower curtain and bending his big body down to make a white patch on the side of the cast-iron tub.

Tina, scrubbing at the pig blood and rinsing away the pink foam, with the taste of lard on her tongue and the sting of the cleaning fluid at the back of her throat, felt queasy and light-headed. She sensed Uncle standing behind her in the doorway, watching her. When she finished and straightened up, she turned around to look at him, but nobody was there.

On the third day, she unpacked. She placed her valuables—her money and her passport—in the drawer of her bedside table. She put her clean clothes in the chest of drawers and her laundry in the wicker basket.

Grandmother did the family's washing in a big, metal tub with a corrugated board and a bar of soap, and then she threw the dirty water out of the front door. It dashed on the steps and hit the slabs four floors below, and dried in the sun. The sometimes damp pram was kept at the bottom of the staircase. Every trip out was four flights down and four flights back up carrying the baby. Tina seemed to be forever on those slick steps with the baby in her arms.

Grandmother showed her how to scrub the men's shirts against the washboard, how to hang them out to dry on the lines strung from window to window, and how to cook pulled pork. At suppertime, Father sat down quickly and ate hungrily.

'You made his favourite,' said Uncle.

Grandmother touched her on the arm and said something which Uncle translated. 'She says you can be his girlfriend,' he said, indicating Father, who did not look up from his meal. Tina laughed before she realised that Grandmother was making a genuine proposition. Grandmother spoke again, and Uncle said, 'She says if you do not like him, you can be my girlfriend.' He did not smile.

'But you have a girlfriend,' she said.

'She lives in London,' he said. 'You can live here.'

After supper, after the pork scraps had been scraped into the dog's bowl and the greasy plates had been washed and dried and put away, Tina went outside to watch the day ending. The bone-dry washing hung in the sultry air, the dusk beginning to settle in its folds. Uncle was sitting on the top step of the staircase, eating a bag of aniseed balls. She sat down beside him and asked, 'Where is the baby's mother?'

For a long minute, he did not answer or look at her. He moved an aniseed ball around in his mouth; she heard it clattering against his teeth. He rubbed at the dark circles under his eyes. And then he said, 'She left.'

'She left her baby?'

'She tried to take the baby.'

'Where is she?'

He worked the aniseed ball until it was nothing, and then he looked at her and said, 'She's gone.' He smiled; she saw his teeth, his saliva stained red, and the flash of a flat cut diamond on his incisor.

'But without the baby?'

'A man must have an heir,' he said. He put another aniseed ball in his mouth and did not look at her again.

She wondered about the diamond; she wondered whether it rubbed against the inside of his lip, and whether it hurt. She could almost taste the blood.

Every other evening, when the baby was asleep, Tina had a bath. She took very little hot water, not wanting an incomprehensible scolding from Grandmother, nor a comprehensible one from Uncle. She sat in the deep tub with lukewarm water lapping at her bare knees, bathing warily. There was no lock on the bathroom door. At first she pulled the shower curtain across, in case anybody should come in by mistake, but she found that she preferred to leave the curtain drawn back, so that she could see there was nobody there.

Halfway up the iron staircase, she pauses. She stands still, her arms aching, her legs shaking, nausea swelling in her stomach. She listens to the distant buzz of life, the sounds coming from the market and the factory—a noisy, windowless box of a building in which Uncle works on the production line. She has often wondered what it would be like to spend so much of your life like that, without daylight, without sunshine, without fresh air. The night shift has ended and the day shift has started, and Uncle will be home soon. A mile away, the road is choked with cars and buses, and the streets are full of people coming and going. But here, now, it is dreadfully quiet.

They watched her as she went about the house. They were watching when she went out and they were watching when she returned.

She went to the kitchen to make Father a cup of tea and found Grandmother and Uncle in there. While she filled and boiled the kettle, and fetched a cup and saucer from the cupboard, and made the sweet, black tea, she felt their eyes on her back, felt their gaze following her as she carried the full, hot cup slowly across the kitchen and down the steps. She recalled reading somewhere that if a woman is carrying a cup of tea down the stairs and falls, she won't drop the cup because she will think it's a baby. As Tina stepped carefully from the bottom stair into the hallway, Uncle, close behind her, said, 'She wants to know if you have children.' Tina turned, and the cup rattled on its saucer.

Tina looked at Grandmother, who was standing behind Uncle in the kitchen doorway looking at her, at her figure, at her hips.

'No,' said Tina. 'No children.'

Grandmother spoke, and then Uncle said, 'But you can have children, yes?'

Tina hesitated, thrown, but she said, 'Yes,' although she wondered how she would know—she didn't know that she *couldn't* have children.

In the living room, she gave the cup of tea to Father and he watched her pick up the baby, who smelt of cigarettes.

She gave the baby a bath in the big tub, crouching on the concrete floor, while Grandmother sat on the toilet seat lid with a towel, looking at her. It made Tina nervous, being stared at like that. Grandmother's gaze made her clumsy, made the baby feel particularly slippery and squirmy. He tipped out of the cradle of her arm and headbutted the surface of the water before she righted him. Grandmother stood quickly and, scolding her, intervened, taking the baby out of the bath, out of Tina's hands. She wrapped him in the towel and jiggled him up and down, and he began to cry. Tina drained the shallow bath, and the baby's jagged crying became screaming, scratching at her raw nerves.

One evening, carrying a full glass of water down the kitchen steps, Tina stumbled. The heavy, cut-glass tumbler fell out of her hand, clipped the stone step and whumped down on the carpet, where it lay in the dark puddle of its own spillage. She inspected the glass, and found a crack. There was nobody around — nobody in the hallway, nobody in the kitchen. Tina dried the wet patch on the carpet as best she could and put the glass at the back of the cupboard, behind the rest of the tumblers.

Later, walking through the market, stopping to look at a stall full of glassware, she saw some tumblers very similar to Grandmother's, though not quite the same. She decided she would buy one and secretly replace the one she had dropped, but when she looked in her purse she found she had only small change. She went back to the flat to fetch more of her money, but when she opened the drawer of her bedside table it was empty, her valuables gone.

She went to confront Grandmother, who pretended not to understand her, dismissing her with a flicking, shooing hand. Tina turned to Uncle, who said, 'We will keep safe your money and your passport.' Tina tried to argue, to insist that they return her possessions, but Uncle calmly repeated, 'We will keep safe the valuable things.'

She sat quietly through supper, her stomach knotted, unable to eat. She did not know what she could do, apart from going into their bedrooms to look for her belongings, but there was always someone in the house.

When everyone had finished, Tina cleared away the dirty dishes, scraping the uneaten pork from her plate. Grandmother and the men remained at the table, talking and watching her. Tina washed up. She did not care now about the glass she had broken and hidden in the cupboard. She handled the cut glass tumblers roughly — they clinked in the water and squeaked in her wet hands in mid-air. Grandmother spoke sharply to Uncle, who said to Tina, 'They are heirlooms. They are valuable.' He thumped his fist twice against his big chest, against his heart, to suggest their sentimental value.

Tina dried the glasses and opened the cupboard to put them away, and immediately she could see that the one she had pushed to the back was gone.

'We must say, Tina,' said Uncle, 'when we make a mistake.'

She put the baby to bed, lingering long after he fell asleep. She couldn't bear to go back to the smoky, suffocating kitchen. Her top was wet under the armpits. Her back and her scalp were sweating. She went to the bathroom, ran the cold tap, and splashed lukewarm water on her face. She opened the tiny window wide, hoping for a little air, but instead she felt the day's warmth slumping through like dead weight.

She nears the top of the iron staircase, and now she is climbing so slowly but still she is almost there.

She went from the bathroom to her bedroom and stopped outside the door. She looked back towards the kitchen, where they were all busy talking, and then stepped across the hallway and slowly opened Grandmother's bedroom door. The baby was asleep in his cot, with his night-light on. She crossed the quiet room, hearing the noise of the carpet beneath her feet. She went first to Grandmother's bedside table and opened the drawer, but inside there was just a Bible. She slid her hand under the mattress and ran it all the way down to the foot of the bed, feeling the bare slats. Under the bed, there were only slippers; in the chest of drawers there were only clothes.

Tina went to the cot. She slipped her fingers down

between the bars and the baby's mattress. The baby sighed and Tina froze, willing him not to wake, not to cry—she did not want Grandmother coming down the hallway. She wondered whether she dared to look in the room the men shared. She could still hear the debate going on in the kitchen.

Suddenly, she looked up. A figure stood in the doorway, looking at her with her hands in the baby's cot. Her heart bucked inside her chest like a wild horse roped.

'I was just checking on the baby,' said Tina, and her voice sounded strange to her, disembodied in the dim room.

'My mother does not like you,' said Uncle, the diamond glinting on his tooth as he spoke. 'She does not trust you.'

Tina wondered how long he had been standing there.

'I want my things back,' she said.

'You do not need your passport now,' he said. 'But I will bring you money.'

Tina went to her room and sat on the edge of her bed. When there was a knock at her door, she went and opened it. Uncle held out a couple of notes in the local currency, just pocket money. She looked at him, and he said, 'It is enough now. Why do you want more?'

She took the notes, and closed her door again.

It was so hot. It was unbearable. The window in her room did not open; the frame appeared to have been painted shut. But it seemed that there was no cool air anyway, anywhere. Her heart was beating fast and she felt nauseous. Her mouth was dry; she wanted a glass of water but she did not want to leave her room. She got into bed and lay awake, sweating into these strangers' sheets, loathing the dragging summer, just wanting it to end.

In the morning, she took the baby out early, and quietly, leaving Grandmother sleeping. She walked him slowly through the market while it was setting up, and through the still-calm streets, delaying her return. He fell asleep, and she thought that she would have liked to just keep walking, walking with the dozing baby, never to go back.

She stopped at a payphone and thought of calling her parents. She had coins, or she could reverse the charges. She put the brake on the pram, lifted the receiver, and dialled the international number. It rang—she saw the phone at home ringing in the empty kitchen, ringing through the dark house, because, she realised, if it was early morning here then it was very early at home, still nighttime. She pictured her parents asleep in their bed, or half-woken, frowning into their pillows and turning over. She stood with the receiver pressed to her ear long after she knew that nobody was going to answer.

She heard the factory whistle blow, signalling the end of the night shift. Now Uncle would go drinking, and then he would return home for breakfast.

She replaced the receiver and collected her returned coins. She walked back through the market, and saw the glassware stall again. She had her pocket money from Uncle in her purse. She stopped and looked at the cut glass tumblers which were not too different from the one she had damaged. She bought one, as a peace offering, and then she walked slowly back to the flats.

She parked the pram on the wet slabs underneath the iron staircase. Grandmother was up—she had done a wash already. Damp laundry hung in the morning sunshine. Tina lifted the sleepy baby out of the pram and began the climb up to the top. She felt queasy at the thought of sitting down to breakfast. She had no appetite. She had a twitch under her eye.

She was more than halfway up when she realised she had left the glass from the market in the bottom of the pram. Wanting to give it to Grandmother before breakfast, she started back down, down the slick steps with the baby in her arms, and perhaps it was because she had not slept or eaten; perhaps it was because she felt sick and was too hot; perhaps it was because she was hurrying, not wanting to meet Uncle on the stairs, smelling of alcohol and aniseed; but in any case, she tripped.

At the top of the staircase, she takes the weight in the crook of one arm and, with a deep breath, opens the door with her free hand. She steps into the bright hallway and pulls the door to behind her, and when the door closes, it is dark.

# SALLEY VICKERS

# Epiphany

THE MAROON-AND-CREAM country bus, the only one that ran that day on account of it being the holiday season, was late and it was already dark when the young man reached the crossroads at the top of the hill. Before him, the lights of the town cascaded into the creased steel of the water below. Way out, at the furthest reach of his vision, a fishing boat was trawling the horizon, carrying with it a frail cargo of two beads of greenish light.

It was colder than he had bargained for and he missed a scarf as he walked downhill towards the sea. The road was as familiar to his feet as to his mind. Maybe more so; the body has its own memory.

He had walked there so often as a child, envisaging the world he was going to escape to, a world wide with promise, a match for his elastic imagination. 'Charlie,' his gran used to say, 'is made for better things than here.'

A cat slithered past his legs, a strip of skinny orange fur, and he wondered what 'better' meant to his gran. Fast cars and manicured blondes well turned out, in nightclubs, probably. Long ago, his gran had been a dancer herself, and in marrying a fisherman had come down in the world, in her own eyes.

He had been brought up, mostly, by his gran as he didn't have a father to speak of. And his mother had had to work. Then a time came, he couldn't be quite sure when, when Ivor, a furniture remover who drove a van, appeared on the scene. He came round for Sunday lunch, which they never usually had, and his mother had smacked his leg because he had revealed it was the first time he had eaten pork roast. She married Ivor in the end and he gave his stepson his name, McGowan, and a measure of grudging security. But Charlie always knew that his real father would have been different.

At the bottom of the hill, he turned right along the promenade, which ran alongside the unmindful water. Wrought-iron lampposts shed a lofty and undiscriminating light on a man peeing. The man shuffled round, setting his back towards Charlie, making a token gesture towards an embarrassment which neither of them felt.

Charlie continued along the promenade until it began to veer back towards the town and then ducked under the railings, and waded through inhospitable pebbles towards a hut, where, in the summer, ice cream and confectionary and hot dogs were sold. He leaned his back against the shuttered little structure and lit a cigarette, waiting.

He had smoked two cigarettes and was lighting a third before a car came to a stop in the road beside the hut. The door banged to and then the heavy crunching tread of a dark shape of a man came towards him.

For a moment, Charlie thought the man was aiming a gun at him, then he realised it was a hand. He took the hand warily and shook it.

'Charles?'

'Charlie. Charles if you like.'

'Charlie then. I found you.'

'Yes.'

'Shall we walk, Charlie?'

They walked along the pebbled shore while the waves made audible little flirtatious sallies and withdrawals at their feet.

'You like the sea?' The voice was deep but awkwardness made it rise unnaturally.

'It's OK. You get tired of it, growing up beside it.'

'I never did.' There was a tint of reproach in the voice now.

'You live beside the sea, then?'

'I live by it. Your mum not tell you I was a fisherman?'

'She never told me anything about you.'

'Can't say I blame her. She was all right, your mum. A firebrand.' It wasn't easy, Charlie thought, talking to a man you'd never met whose face you couldn't even see. 'How did you find me then, if your mum told you nothing?'

'My gran kept an address.'

'Ah, she liked me, your gran. I sent you presents, birthday and Christmas.'

'When's my birthday, then?' Charlie said, hoping to catch him out.

'May twelfth, five fifteen in the morning, just in time to meet the morning catch.'

'I never got any presents.'

'I did wonder.'

Behind them, along the promenade, a car hooted and the harsh voices of some youths rang out, 'Fuck you!' 'Fuckin' madman! Fuck it!' 'Fuck off!'

'Language,' said the man walking beside Charlie. It was hard to tell whether the comment was a reproof or merely an observation.

'Mum never let me swear.'

It wasn't true. But he felt a weird obligation to assert

a spurious vigilance on his mother's part, to distance her from this discovered act of treachery. For more years than he could bear to calculate, he had longed for some token from his father. The news that this had been denied him, deliberately withheld, prompted a general defensiveness.

'She was all right, your mum.'

Charlie detected that this was the man's mantra against some cause for bitterness and tact made him draw back for a moment before lobbing the question: 'Why d'you leave her then?'

'That what she told you?'

In a moment of unspoken agreement, they had stopped and were looking out over the sea. The slate surface shimmered provocatively under the beam of the lamps on the long posts and the diffused lights of the windows of the bungalows, way up on Fulborough Heights.

'She say I left her, then?' the man asked again. There was an undertow of something in his voice Charlie recognised.

'Didn't you?' Any notion that there could be doubt over this was fantastic. He had been raised in the sure and certain knowledge that he had an absconding father. And yet there was that pleading animal tone.

'She chucked me out.'

'What for?' Relief that there might be another explanation for his father's dereliction struggled with the stronger fear that he was going to be asked to accommodate worse news.

'Didn't rate me, I guess.'

They had reached the farthest point of the beach's curve and, with the same accord with which they had stood surveying the dappled waves, the two men turned to walk back the way they had come. Charlie dug his hands in his pockets against the wind, conscious as he did so that he was adopting a pose he had absorbed from films. The gesture was a feeble understudy for the words needed to voice what he was feeling.

'Your dad was a right bastard,' he had heard his mother declare time and again. 'Walked out and left me with a bawling kid to cope with. Mind you,' she had added, when the black mood was on her, 'the way you go on, you'd have driven him out even if he hadn't gone before.'

'Your mum's mum, your gran, wanted me to stay,' the man who was his father resumed. 'Maybe I should've. I've often wondered what was right.'

'Yes,' Charlie said. 'Maybe you should.' As he said it he was aware of a dreadful gratitude emanating from the presence beside him. It seemed bizarre to make someone glad to learn that they had not done what you ardently wished they had done.

'You missed me, then?' The voice was now unquestionably wistful.

'Yeah, I missed you,' Charlie consented. He felt sick at his own words.

'Missed' wasn't the size of it. He had mourned his absent father, fiercely, inconsolably, endlessly, desperately. Since he could remember thinking his own thoughts, missing his father had taken the lion's share of his inner life. It was, he suddenly recognised, to seek his father that he had made his way to London, for the only way to bear the loss had been to conjure that impossibly glamorous figure, whose flight it was possible to condone on grounds of innate superiority. He could never have envisaged this hesitant man with the unsettling squeak and tremor in his voice. Sharply, fervently, he wished this newly recovered parent to the bottom of the sea.

'And you are a fisherman?' he said aloud in response

to a solitude he had come, over the years, to resent but had never had the heart to forswear.

'Was is the operative word. I don't do anything now. No work for us fisher folk these days, what with the EEC.'

The note of whimsy was terrible. An unemployed, down-at-heel, shabby fisherman was no substitute for an insouciant profligate high-hearted deserter. Charlie, acute to personal danger, braced himself for further unwanted revelation.

'I live with a decent woman. Pat. She sees me right. Works up at the local pub and helps out with the B and B there. I do odd jobs for them too. We get by. What do you do?'

'I'm an actor.' Pause. 'Well, trying to be. But . . .'

'It's hard, I know. You've got the voice.'

'Have I?' Charlie felt a shot of excitement at this unexpected encouragement.

'A good voice, you've got. I heard it straight away. I had a voice once. Someone put me in a film. Said I was a natural. Offered to take me to Hollywood.'

'Really?' Suspicion of this hint of redeeming enterprise in his lost parent hovered over relief.

'I'm not a liar,' Charlie's father said placidly. They had reached the beach hut again and he stopped and took out a packet of cigarettes. 'Untipped, they are. Got the habit on the boats.'

'Hard to get, aren't they now?'

'I'm not a liar,' his father repeated, cradling the match with which he lit Charlie's cigarette with a big hand. Red lobster hands. 'I didn't leave your mum. She didn't want me. Don't blame her. But I shouldn't have left you.'

Charlie stood, looking out at the glimmer of the receding tide, pulling on his father's cigarette. A strand of tobacco had stuck to his lip. The words he had longed to hear, had rehearsed to himself so often, in bed at night, crying himself to sleep after his mother had been having a go, 'I shouldn't have left you', bounced away into the unpitying darkness. He felt nothing. Not even contempt. It was a poor sort of an offering from a prodigal father.

'I'm glad you've come to see her anyway,' he said at last.

'I'd've come sooner if you'd asked.'

'Yes,' Charlie said. 'I know. I should have asked you before.' It was a kind of acknowledgement between the two of them.

'Better late than never,' said his father. Through the darkness Charlie could just make out that he was grinning. 'Shall we go in my car?'

'I don't have one. I came by bus.'

Walking through the hospital corridors, which smelled of nothing normal, Charlie looked at his father for the first time. Broad shoulders, middle height, hair once dark, now mostly grey, a face which might have been handsome once but had settled into hangdog, jeans, donkey jacket, with a sprinkling of dandruff about the shoulders, visible white vest, plaid wool shirt, brown suede shoes, wrong shade for the rest of what he was wearing. A model of unexceptional ordinariness. Except that he was the father he had never had—and at the same time he was not. He was quite another father. A stranger.

'I bought her a present,' Charlie's new father said, producing a box from his pocket. 'Roses chocolates. Too late for Christmas, but she used to like Roses. Mind you, she liked hard centres best, Jen, but I thought in the circumstances soft centres might go down better.'

Charlie did not say that his mother was past eating anything, even soft centres. Nor did he consciously form the

219

thought, but in the region of his mind, which as yet had formed no words, he became aware that he was in charge of these two beings, his parents. An access of violent tenderness waylaid him and he touched his father's arm. 'She'll be glad you remembered.'

'Think so?' The blue eyes were horribly beseeching. A hurt child's eyes. 'Bit late for Christmas but . . .'

'I'm sure so,' Charlie said, untruthfully. He was not at all sure how his mother would take this. It had been an impulse to follow up the address he had found in his gran's oak bureau when he cleared it after she died. It was written on a corner of torn-off card, which, from the faint trace of glitter, and the suggestion of a robin's breast, looked as if it had been sent one Christmas. He had guessed at once whom the card had come from.

They were approaching his mother's ward, which, in deference to her condition, was shared by only two other patients. 'Both on their way out' as his stepfather had observed. Ivor, Charlie guessed, was counting his wife's definitely numbered days to the time he could settle down to widowerhood and a story of suffering nobly borne.

Charlie's mother's was the first bed in the ward and, as was customary now, she was behind drawn curtains, as if she was rehearsing what it would be like to have the curtains drawn for good.

'Mum?'

'What? Oh, it's you. You're back, then.'

'Mum, I've brought a visitor.'

Across the face, once pretty, now bleached by years of discontent and disappointment, and further diminished by drugs and pain, flashed a sudden enlivening angry interest. 'Who is it?'

Charlie's father stepped forward, jolting the bedside

cupboard so that the jug of water on it rocked perilously. 'It's me, Jen.'

'Mind that jug. Who's "me", when you're at home?'

But she knew. And Charlie knew that she knew. And in that instant he knew that he had done something remarkable. Unquestionably, unmistakably, his mother was pleased. Relief rushed in on him, warming him like a double Scotch on an empty stomach.

'It's Jeff, Jen.'

'My God!'

'No, your Jeff!' For a moment, there was something that Charlie saw in his father's face. Charm.

'I don't believe it!'

'All right if I sit down, Jen?'

'Sit here.' Charlie's father sat on the bed where she had gestured and Charlie saw that his mother's face had grown not pale but pink. 'I don't believe it,' she said again. 'How did you get here?'

'Him.' Charlie's father nodded towards their son. 'He found me. Wrote to me. Said you were ill and . . .'

'I'm dying, you know that, don't you?'

Charlie, who had had strict instructions from his step-father to keep this news from his mother, felt a further rush of absolving relief.

'It's why I came, Jen.'

'He tell you that?' Charlie's mother gestured towards him.

'No. I guessed. You don't mind me coming?'

''Course I don't, you daft 'apeth.'

Charlie said, 'I'm going for a smoke and a wander. I'll be back in a bit.'

He walked down the corridor, where he met the duty sister. 'Mum's got another visitor,' he explained. He didn't want anyone spoiling anything by blundering in with a change of her bag, or whatever.

'That's nice. Who is it?'

'A relative. They've not seen each other in a while.'

'Ah, nice,' the sister said, vaguely benign. 'It's one of the good things about the Christmas season. People get together again who mightn't otherwise.'

She had a point, Charlie granted, staring at the hospital Christmas tree. It was still decked, though it was twelfth night, still bearing brightly wrapped faux presents. His gran would have said it was the devil's luck not to have that all down by now. Or was it the last day they could safely be up before the bad fairies dropped out of the greenery to work their harm? What was it happened today? He'd forgotten. His gran would surely have told him.

He went outside for a smoke and looked at the saucepan in the night sky. We Three Kings of Orientar, he remembered suddenly. On their camels following the star. Bringing gifts, gold, frankincense and . . . he couldn't remember the last one.

When he returned to the ward, his father was still sitting on the bed holding his sleeping mother's hand. She looked peaceful. Myrrh, he suddenly remembered. That was the other one. Myrrh. They put it on dead bodies, his teacher had told them at school. Death had its good side. Because his mother was dying, he'd found his father. But when she was dead and gone he would have to live with the find. Be careful what you look for, you might find it, his gran had sometimes said.

The box of Roses chocolates, like a small wayside altar, stood unopened beside the jug of water on the bedside cupboard.

Noting Charlie's glance, his father said, 'She says she'll have one later.'

'D'you want to go?'

'Better had. Pat'll be . . . But I'll come again, if . . . ?'

'Yeah, sure.'

'I'll bring Pat. That's if . . .'

'Yeah, sure.'

'Perhaps I won't. She didn't mind, did she, Jen, that I came?'

A lifetime of minding. Minding for her as well as for himself. Minding her taunts, her viciousness. Minding her accusations. Minding her furious campaigns against his life, and, almost worse—for there was no way he could help or stop her—her own. Excusing her fits of temper, her cruelty, her unpredictable hysteria because she had suffered this shocking injustice. Was it simply that she'd made a mistake? Sent away a man who loved her and then regretted it? Could she so not acknowledge the enormity of what she had done that she had hidden behind this bogus story, this piece of twisted, pointless, self-justifying confabulation? Or was she just an out and out liar? How could he tell now? He'd had to make a life without his father, and soon he would be making it without his mother. And who were they anyway, his father and his mother? How would he ever know now?

'She was pleased with the chocolates, wasn't she?' his father said. 'She loved chocolates, Jen did. I used to buy them for her: Roses, Quality Street. It wasn't true, you know, about them asking me to Hollywood. I wanted them to. I'd have gone. But I reckon the film wasn't any great shakes after all. And they didn't ask.'

'Yes,' Charlie said. He looked at his father's red lobster hands, clenching and unclenching. 'I expect she was pleased about the chocolates.'

'Yes,' said his father. 'She did seem pleased, didn't she?

# Contributors' Biographies

ALAN BEARD is the author of two short story collections, *Taking Doreen out of the Sky* and *You Don't Have to Say*. He edited *Going the Distance*, an anthology celebrating twenty years of the Tindal Street Fiction Group, and had a story included in *Best Short Stories 1991*. Married with two children, he lives and works in Birmingham.

CHRISTOPHER BURNS is the author of five novels, including *The Condition of Ice* and *Dust Raising*, and a short story collection, *About the Body*. A new novel, *A Division of the Light*, will be published in 2012. He lives with his wife in Whitehaven, west Cumbria.

JOHN BURNSIDE was born in Dunfermline in 1955. He is the author of six novels, including *The Dumb House*, *The Locust Room* and *Glister*, and a collection of short stories, *Burning Elvis*, as well as numerous volumes of poetry and non-fiction. He has been shortlisted for and has won many awards for his fiction and poetry.

SJ BUTLER is a freelance writer and editor living in Sussex. 'The Swimmer' is the first short story she has published.

ROBERT EDRIC is the author of some twenty novels including *A New Ice Age*, *The Book of the Heathen*, *Gathering the Water* and *The London Satyr*. A series of crime novels, *The Song Cycle Trilogy*, was set in Hull, close to the author's home in East Yorkshire.

PHILIP LANGESKOV was born in Copenhagen in 1976. His stories have appeared in *The Decadent Handbook*, *Bad Idea Magazine* and elsewhere. He lives in Norwich.

HEATHER LEACH's short stories have appeared in *Metropolitan*, *The Big Issue*, *The City Life Book of Manchester Stories*, *Northern Stories*, *Mslexia* and elsewhere. She lives in Manchester and is co-editor and writer of two books on creative writing.

KIRSTY LOGAN lives in Glasgow where she edits a literary magazine, teaches creative writing and reviews books. She is working on her first novel, *Little Dead Boys*, and a collection, *The Rental Heart and Other Fairytales*. Her short fiction has been published in numerous anthologies and magazines, and has been broadcast on BBC Radio 4.

BERNIE MCGILL was born in Northern Ireland and lives in Portstewart. 'No Angel' won second prize in both the Seán Ó Faoláin Short Story Competition and the Michael McLaverty Short Story Award. Her short fiction has been broadcast by BBC Radio Ulster and published in magazines and anthologies. Her first novel, *The Butterfly Cabinet*, was published in the UK and Ireland in 2010.

HILARY MANTEL was born in Glossop in 1952. She is the author of ten novels, including *Fludd*, *Beyond Black* and *Wolf Hall*, as well as a collection, *Learning to Talk: Short Stories*, and a memoir, *Giving Up the Ghost*. She has won numerous prizes, among them the 2009 Man Booker Prize for *Wolf Hall*, and in 2006 was made a CBE.

ADAM MAREK won the 2011 Arts Foundation Fellowship in short story writing. His collection, *Instruction Manual for Swallowing*, was long-listed for the Frank O'Connor Prize, and in 2010 he was shortlisted for the inaugural *Sunday Times* EFG Private Bank Short Story Award. He lives in Bedfordshire with his wife and sons.

CLAIRE MASSEY's fiction, poetry and articles have appeared in *Cabinet des Fées*, *Enchanted Conversation*, *Flax*, *Rainy City Stories*, *Magpie Magazine* and *Brittle Star*. She is founder and editor of *New Fairy Tales*. She lives in Lancashire with her husband and two young sons.

ALISON MOORE was born in Manchester. Since 2000 her short stories have been published in magazines and competition anthologies. She has won prizes in Wales and Northern Ireland and has been shortlisted for the Fish Prize, the Bridport Prize and, in 2009, the inaugural Manchester Fiction Prize. She lives in Leicestershire with her husband and young son.

MICHÈLE ROBERTS is a poet, novelist and broadcaster. She has been shortlisted for the Booker prize and is a winner of the WH Smith Literary award. A fellow of the Royal Society of Literature, she is also a Chevalier de l'Ordre des Arts et des Lettres. Born in Hertfordshire to a French mother and English father, Roberts now divides her time between London and Mayenne, France.

DAVID ROSE lives in Middlesex. A co-founder of literary magazine *Main Street Journal*, his short fiction has appeared in a range of magazines and anthologies, as well as a mini-collection, *Stripe*, and a chapbook, *Being a Greek*. Rose's first novel, *Vault*, is forthcoming, to be followed by a short story collection, *Posthumous Stories*.

LEONE ROSS was born in Coventry and grew up in Jamaica. Her short fiction has been widely anthologised in Britain and America. She teaches Creative Writing at Roehampton University in London. She is the author of two novels, *All The Blood Is Red* and *Orange Laughter*. Her next novel *The Inevitability of Strooops* will be published in 2012. 'Love Silk Food' was a runner-up for the 2008 VS Pritchett Memorial Prize.

LEE ROURKE is the author of the novel *The Canal* and the short story collection *Everyday. A Brief History of Fables: From Aesop to Flash Fiction* is forthcoming. He is Contributing Editor for 3:*AM Magazine* and also blogs at *SPONGE!* He lives in London.

DAI VAUGHAN, born in 1933, is a novelist and short story writer with a background in documentary filmmaking. He is the author of the novels *The Cloud Chamber*, *Moritur*, *Totes Meer*, *Non-Return* and *The Treason of the Sparrows*. His short stories are collected in *Germs* and his essays in *For Documentary*. He lives in north-west London.

SALLEY VICKERS is the author of six novels, including *Miss Garnet's Angel*, *Instances of the Number 3*, *The Other Side of You* and *Dancing Backwards*, and a short story collection, *Aphrodite's Hat*. She has worked as a dancer, an artist's model, a university lecturer and a psychoanalyst. She now writes full-time and lives in London and Cambridge.

# Acknowledgements

The editor wishes to thank Mark Richards, Nigel Kendall, Philip Langeskov, Tania Hershman, Gareth Evans, Gerald McEwen, Bill Hamilton.

'Foreigner', copyright © Christopher Burns 2010, was first published in the *Warwick Review*, September 2010, and is reprinted by permission of the author.

'Dinner of the Dead Alumni', copyright © Adam Marek 2010, was first published in *Riptide 5* and is reprinted by permission of the author.

'The Swimmer', copyright © SJ Butler 2010, was first published in the *Warwick Review*, December 2010, and is reprinted by permission of the author.

'So Much Time in a Life', was first published online at www.didsburyartsfestival.com/competition and is reprinted by permission of the author.

'Staff Development', copyright © Alan Beard 2010, was first published in the *Warwick Review*, June 2010, and is reprinted by permission of the author.

'The Rental Heart', copyright © Kirsty Logan 2010, was first published in *Pank* 4, January 2010, and is reprinted by permission of the author.

'Notes on a Love Story', copyright © Philip Langeskov 2010, was first published online in *Five Dials* 9 and is reprinted by permission of the author.

'No Angel', copyright © Bernie McGill 2010, was first published in *Scandal and Other Stories* (Linen Hall Library) and is reprinted by permission of the author.

'Slut's Hair', copyright © John Burnside 2010, was first